I0556718

Adventure In
North Pole

About the Author

Arjit Jha is the Author of this book. This is his first book. His birth date is 07 February 2007 and is presently 12 years old. Arjit has participated in many sports events, his main sport is cricket and table tennis. He has a hobby of reading adventurous novels and sci-fi and fiction novel. His favorite novel is the Amulet set. He studies in class VII in Delhi Public School. He has one older brother Aharnish Jha who studies in Class 9. His parents' names are Rajeev K. Jha and Mamta Jha.

Adventure In North Pole

Arjit Jha

ZORBA BOOKS

ZORBA BOOKS

Publishing Services by Zorba Books, 2019
Website: www.zorbabooks.com
Email: info@zorbabooks.com
Copyright © Arjit Jha

Print Book ISBN: 978-93-88497-86-2
Ebook ISBN: 978-93-88497-87-9

All rights reserved. No part of this book may be reproduced or transmitted in any form or by any means, electronic or mechanical, except by a reviewer. The reviewer may quote brief passages, with attribution, in a review to be printed in a magazine, newspaper, or on the Web—without permission in writing from the copyright owner.

The publisher under the guidance and direction of the author has published the contents in this book, and the publisher takes no responsibility for the contents, it's accuracy, completeness, any inconsistencies, or the statements made. The contents of the book do not reflect the opinion of the publisher or the editor.

The publisher and editor shall not be liable for any errors, omissions, or the reliability of the contents of the book.

Any perceived slight against any person's, place or organization is purely unintentional.

Zorba Books Pvt. Ltd.(opc)

Gurgaon, INDIA

Contents

Foreword vii

Preface ix

Characters In The Story xi

Chapter 1 Trip Idea 1

Chapter 2 Antonio Gets A Smartphone 7

Chapter 3 Antonio & Jayden Discovers The Plan .. 11

Chapter 4 Jayden Gets A Laptop 17

Chapter 5 The Taco-Meco 21

Chapter 6 Mayday! Mayday! Mayday! 27

Chapter 7 Get... Set... Survive 36

Chapter 8 Ben And William Make It Alive 41

Chapter 9 Maximus: The Polar Bear Pet 43

Chapter 10 Sara Knows 49

Chapter 11 The Vampire 51

Chapter 12 Sara Discovers The Helicopter
Change 55

Chapter 13 Survive In A Cave With A Stranger 58

Chapter 14 Satan Lucifer 65

Chapter 15 They Found A Part Of The Helicopter 74

Chapter 16 The Archeologist Figure Out The Plan....79

Chapter 17 The International Supreme Group
Of Villains (Isgv) 86

Chapter 18 Ben Makes a Deal With Satan Lucifer   103

Chapter 19 Sara Gets Help From Air Force 106

Chapter 20 They Found The Flight Fury 112

Chapter 21 Ben's Gotta Live Up To His Deal 127

Chapter 22 Rescue Mission Team 133

Chapter 23 The Platinum Locket 137

Chapter 24 Code Received 144

Chapter 25 They Defeat Satan Lucifer 146

Chapter 26 Home Sweet Home 155

Questions From The Story 157

Foreword

Not every authors novel or book is perfect. Sometime it is hard to write novel or story but that's where you truly need to focus, if you go with the perfect time period, it will be easy if you are writing a book. You have to give it 2 hours, if you write 2 hours daily it will be finished before you know.

I remember writing the book from starting, in 2015, when I started writing in a green diary, I even didn't finished 20 pages then, the next year I again started writing, in 2016, in a rough copy but i gave up. The same happened in the year 2017, because of school I forgot about it, but alas in started writing in 2018 and finally finished it in 2019, so you see everything or anything you do, if it's either write a book, play, dance, sing or even study, you're gonna have to struggle either ways if you do hard work or you don't, every single moment of your life is struggle.

Anything you do find joy in it, don't find depression, to write a book sometimes, I used to angry at every sentence or paragraph, I used find every book in the house and read but in the end it all got me confused and automatically I get frustrated. But if I looked on the bright side I could have rewrite the sentence/paragraph or could thing of something else, the main point is to have fun, otherwise there is no point of doing it.

The main thing and the most important thing is, never ever write a book on a topic which is already taken or never steal other authors ideas that has been used. What's the point of writing a book if you can't imagine or have ideas for it.

Through out my journey I would like to thank my father, Rajeev Jha, he made me what I am today and told me not lose hope, I would also like to thank my mother, Mamta Jha, and my brother, Aharnish Jha, which encourage me to this book, I would sincerely like to thank Manpreet Kaur ma'am, the English Teacher I have studied under.

Arjit Jha

Gurgaon (Haryana)

India

July 2019

Preface

Every adventure in this story is sci-fi, adventure or my wild imagination. My friend and I are really interested in these types of stories. This story is a combination of sci-fi and adventure stories that I have read all my life.

Although my story is based on my imagination many people have suffered the same way in reality too and they have survived it. This book is on them (but not true).

The main objective is to write this for all kids of age 6–12 years. I recommend adults read this, as this story has adventure but some great facts on this topic as well.

The Author
Arjit Jha, 2019

Characters In The Story

ANTONIO: A 17-year-old teen, who is the hero of the story, he is pretty clever. He is really a simple kid who loves his mother and will go to any means to make her happy.

JAYDEN: A 15-year-old teen who is also the hero of the story, he is a comedian, a detective and a hacker. With these abilities he is the only person who owns the most powerful thing in the world, the key to defeat the villain of this story.

MAXIMUS: A polar bear who was healed by Jayden and became his best friend. He helped to defeat the villain of this story.

SATAN LUCIFER: The villain of this story. Generations of his family have been trying to find the hidden place of the sacred stones. But he is unable to do so as long as our hero is alive.

Ben: the hero's stepfather. He doesn't seem to bond with Antonio and Jayden. Even if he tries to go near them, he wouldn't bond even an inch.

William: the pilot of the crashed helicopter, who survives the crash and becomes a part of this adventure.

Sara: the hero's mother who had the idea to send them on a trip together so they all could bond.

Stephen: A person who is a part of the organization called *HOE (HOLDER'S OF EARTH)* which is an organization that stops the bad guys. And an ally who helps Jayden and Antonio.

Adam: an ally who helps Jayden and Antonio by working side-by-side with Satan Lucifer.

Ethan: the rescue mission team's head who help's Sara in finding her two sons and her husband.

Chapter 1
TRIP IDEA

As they say …
There is a city named Iqaluit. It is also the capital of the Canadian territory of Nunavut. The population of Iqaluit is 7,740. Amongst all these people, there lived a family. In the family, there lived two boys. Their names were Antonio and Jayden. Antonio was 17 and Jayden was 15. Antonio was older than Jayden. Jayden was the youngest in the family. Antonio was quite smart and clever. He was quite intelligent too, and Jayden…well you could call him many things, a comedian, a hungry teen, but smart was clearly not one of them. He was also quite a trickster. Although he was a huge fan of Sherlock Holmes and other detectives, and was pretty clever at figuring riddles like detectives,

he was also amazing at something else. No one knew about his secret hobby except Antonio. He could hack computers and almost anything else that was electronic.

Nobody in the family, not even Antonio himself, knew that he was the 'Foreseer'. He didn't see anything until all this happened to Jayden and him.

Their mother's name was Sara Lake and their step-father's name was Ben Lake.

Ben Lake was a very successful businessman.

It was winter and it was very cold. Though they had a happy family, Antonio and Jayden weren't very close with their step-father, Ben.

Sara could see that and she put her mind to work. One night, she came up with an idea.

Sara knew how much the children wanted to go on a helicopter ride. So, one night Sara and their step-father talked and Sara said,

"I see that you are not bonding with the children…so I came up with an idea and booked a helicopter ride for the three of you. The helicopter will fly you to uncle Bob and Aunt Olivia's place. This will give the three of you time to bond with each other. Remember one thing, though, if anything happens to my children I will not spare you."

"Ok ma'am, got it. But just to be clear, it is totally not going to work out," Ben told Sara.

Sara invited Antonio and Jayden to a family dinner together.

Although the two boys didn't really want to have a family dinner, there was no option other than to have dinner together.

At the dining table, Sara said, "Hey kids, listen up. I have booked three tickets for a helicopter ride to your uncle Bob and aunt Olivia in Annoatok. Annoatok is in Greenland. You have been there but you were both very little at the time. Also, you're not just going in any helicopter. You are going for a ride on the Thunder Ranger."

"Yes! Finally, we get some time away from Ben," Antonio whispered to Jayden. Jayden whispered back, "And we'll get a chance to sit in a helicopter!" Suddenly, Sara interrupted them, "I know the three of you will have a great time together."

"Say what!" Antonio said, confused.

"Excuse me, did I just hear you say 'three' boys?" Jayden asked.

Sara said "Yes, you heard it right. There's three of you—Jayden, your father and you…"

"Step-father. Ben is not our father," Antonio said.

"Well, Jayden, your step-father, and you will go on the trip."

Hearing this, Jayden went upstairs.

"Why are you not coming?" Antonio asked his mother.

"I won't be able to come because I have some very important work to finish at my office," Sara said.

"I can't even imagine him as a real father. The only reason I am staying with him is because he makes you happy, not us."

On his way upstairs to his room, antonio said "And no one can ever replace my father, EVER! See you!"

Sara gave Ben a serious look.

When Antonio went upstairs he saw Jayden packing his stuff for the trip. Antonio looked confused and asked Jayden, "Jayden, I don't wanna be correct but, are you going on the trip?"

Jayden replied anxiously, "Antonio, I gave it a lot of thought."

"WHAT! YOU WERE ALONE FOR 70 SECONDS JAYDEN," Antonio furiously roared.

"I don't wanna hurt ya but I am going on this trip because it will be a once in a lifetime opportunity. We are actually going to sit in a real helicopter. It's been so long since we met our grandparents, almost 4 years now," Jayden replied.

"Oh! I see. Go ahead but I am not going at any cost," Antonio said.

"Come on, dude! Look at all the helicopter models we've made. Look at the helicopter games we have played. We have waited our entire life for an opportunity to sit in a helicopter. Well, if you don't want to come on this *awesome* trip, it's fine. Oh, I totally forgot about the amazing gifts we get from our grandparents every time we visit them."

Antonio began reminiscing about all the great gifts he had received on his birthday from his uncle and aunt. He began daydreaming about sitting in a helicopter.

Suddenly, he said, "I am coming. I'm just going to pack my stuff." Jayden said, "Duh, I've already done it." "What, how?" antonio asked him strangely. "I knew you were gonna come to the trip, or..." Jayden said. "Or what?" Antonio asked him. "Or you know..... I would have to kidnap you." Jayden said lightly. "WHAT!" Antonio shouted. "Just kidding, calm down." Jayden relaxed him.

"Hey Jayden, what about the 'Ben' thing though?" asked Antonio

"Relax. Who's even gonna pay attention to him?" Jayden remarked.

He continued speaking, "But we have to lie to mom about..." when suddenly the door opened and Sara entered the room. She asked him sternly, "Lie to mom about what?"

"Umm…" Jayden muttered. Antonio interrupted him, "We were just discussing that we will go on the trip with Ben."

"And why did you want to lie to me? Can I know that as well?" Sara asked.

"Umm… because we wanted to surprise you about our decision to go on the trip with Ben," Antonio replied.

"Aww…that's so sweet of you guys. You really care about me." Sara said. "You have no idea." Jayden thought.

"Have you packed your stuff" asked sara.

"Yup, already done. Mum, when is our flight and what time?" asked Antonio.

"It is day after tomorrow. So, that means it's on Friday at 3'o clock," Sara answered.

"Got it!" said Antonio. After she left the room, they both looked at each other with relieved expressions on their faces.

Suddenly, Sara opened the door and asked "Are you guys hungry? You left the table without finishing your food."

"Nah, we're good," Antonio remarked.

Chapter 2

ANTONIO GETS A SMARTPHONE

After their mother left, Antonio went to the door to check. He didn't see anyone, but unfortunately Ben saw him and called him downstairs. He asked Antonio, "Everything that happened at the dining table, everything that you said about me, were you serious about it?"

"Ah…yes, I was serious about it," Antonio replied. Jayden turned around to return to his room when Ben said, "Okay. In that case, I guess neither of you are coming on the trip with me."

Antonio turned around and said, "Duh…we are both coming on the trip with you. We don't have a choice, but this is the first and last time I am going anywhere with you."

"Well, in that case, I hope we will have a lot of fun together," Ben said.

"I wish not," Antonio muttered to himself while walking upstairs.

"Antonio, just one more thing. Why were you peeking out of your door like that?" Ben asked strangely.

"It is none of your business, Ben" Antonio replied.

"Wow…the kid really hates me," Ben thought.

When he returned to his room, he was shocked to find Jayden missing. He searched for him in all the places where he generally hides in the room but he couldn't find Jayden. He finally found Jayden in the games room packing his video games and his playing stuff and other things.

Antonio noticed his mom in the kitchen cooking something delicious. He went to the kitchen and said to her, "Hey mom! What are you making? I am sure whatever it is it will taste much better than it looks."

"Just speak up. What do you want?" Sara asked.

"Mom, I know I am 17 and not 18 but can I have an X10 mobile phone during the trip only, please?" Antonio asked her.

"The answer is NO," Sara replied.

"But it could be a great help you know. For instance, we can call you anytime or if there is any emergency," Antonio explained.

"You can use Ben's phone if you need," Sara replied.

"Who's gonna use that jerk's phone—I mean what if he's not there at that time? And he can't give us his phone to use all the time."

Sara replied, "In that case, you can use your grandfather's phone."

"Oh come on, mom, please. Just this once. I promise," Antonio requested.

"Well, fine, take it but only for the duration of the trip. You have to return the mobile after the trip, Sara said.

"No mobile after the trip. Got it!"

She pulled out a mobile out of her apron pocket.

Antonio was shocked and said, "It was hidden in your apron's pocket all this time? I have searched for this phone everywhere. I even searched for it in your personal locker—"

"You did what?!" Sara shouted at him.

"Have you even taken money out of the locker?"

"Pfft!!! YES…I mean, NO. I haven't taken any money," Antonio said.

"Okay! But there are some Terms and Conditions before you get this mobile for the trip—" Sara said. She continued "So first come the terms—

1. You have to share this mobile with Jayden.
2. You will not be on this mobile the entire day.
3. No texting with any of your friends. No chatting either until night.
4. Do not open the mobile while you are in the helicopter.

And that's all, for this."

Antonio said "Well I think that is fair—."

"That is so not fair," Jayden interrupted them, "You cannot seriously give such a big responsibility to Antonio. I mean, he loses everything he takes with him. That is his speciality."

"Calm down. I have only allowed him to take the mobile for the duration of the trip." Sara said

"Well other way HOW COULD NOT YOU TELL ME YOU'RE MAKING DOUGHNUTS! You are such a bad mother."

He reached out for some doughnuts when Antonio said to irritate him, "Yoo hoo Jayden, I have the X10 mobile!!!"

But Jayden didn't seem irritated at all.

He remarked, "Oh, I don't care." Saying this he went to the vedio game room and continue packing his games.

Chapter 3

ANTONIO & JAYDEN
DISCOVERS THE PLAN

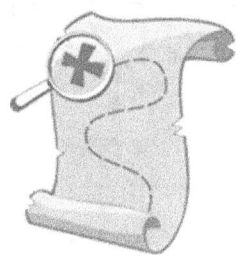

The next day, Antonio woke up in the morning. He yawned and got out of bed. He changed his clothes and went downstairs. He saw that there was no one but Jayden there. He went downstairs and asked Jayden, "What is the time?"

"It is 10:30," Jayden replied.

"Where is everybody else?" Antonio asked.

"They went to the market. They have to buy some stuff for Ben for the trip."

They were both very excited about riding in a helicopter.

Suddenly, they heard someone whispering outside. They were surprised to hear their mom's voice. They tried to go closer so they could hear Ben and Sara's conversation more clearly.

"You have to try to make an effort. This is your chance. Try to bond with them, you know, that's why I am only sending the three of you for the trip. You got to do it."

"But Sara, those kids really hate me. This is really not going to work," Ben said confidently.

"I don't know anything. The only thing I know is that you have to make it work.

"She doesn't know anything. She doesn't even know us. What sort of a mother is she?" Jayden said unacceptably. Antonio told him to stay quiet. But Ben and Sara finished speaking and opened the gate. The house was exactly as they had left it. She saw Antonio and Jayden sitting on the sofa, relaxing. She was surprised to see Antonio awake. They both ran towards the stuff and forgot about everything else. Unfortunately, they were very disappointed because they could not find anything exciting. There were only some warm clothes and blankets. They were pretty upset. They went to their room. Both of them started thinking about the trip. "How can she do that? Does she think that she can send us on a trip with Ben and we will go and bond with him so easily?" Antonio said angrily.

"What…no! She is trying to give him her credit," Jayden said.

"How?" Antonio asked. "She's using food, of course. She will make some yummy food like pizza or tacos or doughnuts, then she'll tell us that Ben made it. Like I said, such a bad mother," Jayden said.

"What! No. Mom is sending the three of us together so that we can bond with ben," Antonio explained.

"Oh! But I've still got a point," Jayden said.

Suddenly, the door opened and Ben came inside. Antonio whispered in Jayden's ear, "What is he doing in our room?"

Jayden replied, "I think he has come here to chat with us and find out something, I suppose."

"You guys know that I can hear you, right?" Ben said.

"Well, we didn't know until now, I guess," Antonio said with an awkward smile.

Ben continued speaking, "Well, okay. I know you guys have gone through a lot since your father passed away—" Antonio interrupted him, "Please. If you are here to tell us about our dad's story, please get out of here then."

"Okay. All I wanted to say is that I know no one can replace your father. I can never take his place. But I don't want either of you to feel that you don't have a father," Ben said emotionally.

"For the first time his words really meant something to me," Jayden said.

"Yeah, me too." Antonio replied. "And I hate it, Ugh...Jesus."

Both of them were lying on the bed when suddenly, Antonio had a vision—Jayden and he were on thin snow and the flight fury was crashing into the woods. They were all alone. He was shocked for a minute but he didn't mention anything to Jayden.

Ben went down to the kitchen and said happily, "I think it worked!"

"Really? You said exactly what I told you to. Am I right?" Sara said excitedly

"Well...no!" Ben replied.

"What did you do there?" Sara shouted. Her voice reached Jayden and Antonio who were still in their room. They silently came outside to see what Ben and Sara were discussing. They didn't interrupt them while they were talking. Instead they continued listening to their conversation.

"He didn't let me finish, forget finish, he didn't even let me start properly," Ben blamed Antonio.

"Ben. This was your chance to get close to them. How could you blow it?" Sara asked him angrily.

"Believe me. It will work out," Ben said.

She trusted Ben and stayed calm and believed him. Antonio and Jayden went to their room. Both of them settled down. Both of them were pretty disappointed with their mother. Antonio suddenly came up with an idea and stood up. He started speaking to Jayden when he realized it was no use because Jayden was already asleep. Antonio was very angry and shouted at him, "Jayden, wake up!"

"Let me sleep, it's midnight. Don't try to wake me up. I am sleeping very deeply I can't even speak," Jayden said while sleeping.

"The first thing is, it is not even evening yet, and the second thing is you are talking while you are sleeping."

Unfortunately, Jayden had to wake up and said, "Whatever you have to say should be worth it because I don't like people waking me up."

Jayden replied, "Fine. I came up with an idea. If we bond with Ben we will get into a lot of trouble."

Antonio asked him, "So what's the idea?"

"We have to tease and trouble him more than he could ever imagine," Antonio explained.

Jayden thought to himself, "Am I the only normal one in this family?"

Chapter 4

Jayden Gets A Laptop

A t night, during dinner

Sara asked, "Have you guys packed everything you need for the trip?"

"Well you can say 99.9% of it," Jayden said

"And what is the remaining 0.1%?" Sara asked him.

"Well there is something I wanna talk to you about mom," Jayden said.

"Hmm…what is it Jayden?" Sara asked giving him a strange look.

"Well, since Antonio has his own mobile for the trip, I think I should also have an electronic gadget for the trip," Jayden replied.

And which electronic gadget would you like to take with you? I mean there are so many gadgets in the house," Sara said.

"In that case, I guess I would like to take the laptop," Jayden replied.

"Nah, you can't take it," Sara said, "I have already given both of you a mobile, haven't I?"

"Oh, come on, mom! I really want to take it on the trip," Jayden requested her.

"Okay, you can take it but then I will have to take the X10 mobile back. Should I take it back?" Sara asked.

"No," Jayden replied sadly.

"Discussion is over. You are not allowed to take the laptop with you," Sara said.

Jayden disappointly headed towards his room.

At that very moment Ben had an idea. He stood up and said, "Okay, Jayden. You can take the laptop. I'll talk to your mom."

"Really, can I? Oh yes, I love you so much," Jayden said.

As soon as the words escaped his mouth, he thought, "Did I just say I love him? Oh, curse my tongue! Now I have to act like I love him or they both will get sad."

Sara was quite touched after hearing what Jayden said. She could not refuse him. She said,

"Fine. You can take the laptop but there are some terms and conditions.

So first come the terms—

1. You have to share this laptop with Antonio.
2. You will not play on the laptop all day.
3. No texting any of your friends and no checking my mail either.

And the conditions—
No watching movies
Do not open the laptop in the helicopter.
And that's all."

While they were going upstairs Ben said to them, "Kids. Do me a favour and check your stuff."

"Okay," Jayden said.

They went back to their room.

"Dude. You are in big trouble," Antonio warned him.

"Yes, I know. Now I have to pretend that I actually like Ben," Jayden said.

"And not just in front of him. You also have to act in front of mom, and if anything goes wrong, Ben's heart will be crushed. If his heart is crushed, then mom will be hurt as well," Antonio warned him.

"Yeah, you have a point, but just get over it for now. We'll see what happens in the future," Jayden said.

They checked their packing once more. They were sitting idly doing nothing, just waiting, waiting for the laptop. Seconds passed, minutes passed, but no sign of the laptop. Suddenly, the door opened and Sara came inside the room holding the laptop in her hands. She gently gave it to Jayden.

There was no space left in their suitcase, so Jayden took the laptop and put it in his school bag.

Chapter 5

THE TACO-MECO

The next day, the day finally arrived for their first helicopter flight. Antonio yawned and opened his eyes and turned his face to the clock to check the time. As soon as he saw the time on the clock, he quickly jumped out of bed as it was already 11:30 AM. He saw that everybody was already awake as usual. He got ready quickly and joined Ben and Jayden downstairs. All of them were ready to go. Finally, they left the house at 12:30 p.m. just as they had planned. Sara kissed their cheeks and bid them goodbye. As they were leaving, Sara prayed they would take advantage of this opportunity and bond.

They were on their way to the airport. Ben was still happy about last night. He couldn't get over his happiness.

Antonio and Jayden were pretty excited about the trip too! While they were going to the airport Jayden said, "We're only going to put the luggage in the transport machine and we'll keep the laptop bag in the helicopter."

"Ok, Jayden!"

Although Ben wasn't sure about this idea he agreed with Jayden anyway.

They reached the airport half an hour earlier, so now all they had to do was wait in the waiting section.

Jayden sang very sorely while they headed to the waiting section.

"Please spare us. Don't dare sing that song, EVER AGAIN! It will start giving me nightmares," Antonio said annoyingly. But he wasn't aware that it was just the beginning of the worst! Antonio kept glancing at his watch to check if 30 minutes had already passed. Ten minutes later, Jayden couldn't stand it any longer and said to Ben, "Ben, I need to go to the washroom. Please tell me the way to the washroom in under 5 seconds or it will be too late and I will pee in my pants."

Ben told him the way in exactly 5 seconds as Jayden had requested. Jayden reacted with his mouth open and mind blank.

"What!? You asked me to tell you the way in 5 seconds."

Finally, Ben told Jayden the way. After Jayden exited the washroom, he accidentally went in the wrong direction and didn't notice it. He kept walking in the wrong direction and finally ended up in front of a wall and realized he had gone off in the wrong direction. He randomly ran around in various directions without any idea where he was going. Suddenly, when he got tired and was beginning to give up, he was surprised to notice a restaurant and not just any restaurant. It was the Taco-Meco restaurant! Luckily, he found Ben and Antonio. They were just a little ahead of the shop. He ran to them huffing and puffing.

Antonio said, "Whoa, whoa! Slow down bud. Catch your breath first."

"There's no time for this," Jayden squeaked while huffing and puffing, "I saw it!"

"You saw what?" Antonio asked.

"I saw the TACO-MECO!!!"Jayden screamed excitedly.

"No way!" Antonio exclaimed.

"C'mon, Ben. What are you waiting for?" Jayden asked.

"Sorry, kids. No can do. It's been 15 minutes already. We have to get to the heliport," Ben said.

"Oh, c'mon!" Jayden said.

As they were heading towards the heliport, suddenly the cloud burst with thunder and it started raining. Ben turned around and Jayden gave him a strange look.

Ben knew the strange look.

Without saying anything, Ben led the way to the restaurant. They went inside the restaurant. The waiter showed them their seats. He gave them the best seats in the restaurant. Their seat was just next to the helicopter's stand.

"Whoa!" Jayden cried.

"Oh, come on! Where is the waiter? I am hungry," Jayden complained.

"Hold on Jayden. He will be here soon."

As Ben had just said, the waiter came soon and he asked them for their order, "Your order, sir?"

Before anyone could say anything, Jayden spoke up, "I want five tacos, two cheese pizzas, three hamburgers, one plate of snacks, one plate nachos and a soft drink."

"We talked about eating, not about buying a banquet!" Antonio told him

"Sorry, sir. We are out of cheese pizzas and hamburgers. The snacks finished just a few minutes earlier," The waiter said awkwardly.

"Seriously, I mean what is this place," Jayden said. He was very disappointed.

"I can't fill my stomach with only tacos and nachos."

"Sorry, sir. This is why our restaurant's name is Taco Meco." The waiter explained.

"Fine, then! Just bring me some plates of tacos and nachos," Jayden told him.

"How many more billion thousand years is he gonna take to serve us???" Jayden said impatiently.

"It has only been five minutes! Man! You have some serious problems with patience…or something," Antonio told him while looking at the helicopters. He continued speaking, "It's been raining for a very a long time. It hasn't rained like this in Iqaluit for two months. I don't know but I have a bad feeling about this."

He hadn't ignored the vision he had had earlier though.

Finally, the waiter served them but Jayden was as unlucky. As soon as he took a taco, Antonio knocked him on his shoulder. He replied "Gah! Let me eat in peace."

As he reached out for the taco again, Antonio knocked him on his shoulder again!

Jayden yelled at him, "Don't disturb me. Especially when I am eating."

As he continued eating his taco, Antonio knocked his shoulder again. This time Jayden shouted at him very, very angrily "WHAT IS IT?"

Antonio calmly pointed towards the window to show him that it had stopped raining.

His mouth opened wide and said "Seriously! Why this does always happen to me. Now we have to go to the—"

"Heliport. We should be going to the heliport now as it isn't raining anymore," Ben said to Jayden giving him a weird look.

"Fine, let's go but before I go, can I eat at least one plate of tacos?" Jayden asked.

"NO," Antonio shouted at Jayden.

"But—"

Jayden couldn't finish his sentence because Antonio interrupted him saying, "no if's and but's" Antonio said.

"Fine, then. You evil monstrous teenager, but I am taking a few tacos. Oh yes, mister, you heard it. I am taking a few of the tacos and you can't stop me from doing that," Jayden told him.

But Ben wasn't interested in their fighting at all. He told them that they had to leave or they wouldn't reach the heliport in time.

So, they left the restaurant at once and headed towards the heliport.

Chapter 6

MAYDAY! MAYDAY! MAYDAY!

After they reached the heliport, the pilot, Mr. William, arrived and he said, "We are extremely sorry sir, we have 'BN' and 'GN'."

"Well, would you mind telling me what 'BN' and 'GN' mean?" Ben asked.

"Oh, it is bad news and good news," The pilot responded.

Out of nowhere, Jayden interrupted, "Oh dear pilot, why don't you ever learn that there is no such thing as bad news or good news?"

"Okay, then. I guess I should just tell you the news. We can't take the THUNDER RANGER due to some technical snags. There has been some trouble with the helicopter and we have been informed that we cannot take any risk."

"THAT IS THE WORST NEWS EVER!" Jayden roared

"Now who has to learn, huh?!" Antonio teased him.

Jayden asked him angrily, "What could the good news be in this kind of situation?"

"Well, we will now be flying in the FLIGHTFURY."

"Yeah like we're gonna believe your lie!" Antonio said, hardly believing him.

"Well then you can see for yourself," the pilot told them.

As he moved away, the first thing they saw was A HUGE RED COLOURED HELICOPTER WITH TRIPLE SIZED WINGS. IT WAS THE MOST AMAZING AND WELL DESIGNED HELICOPTER KNOWN AS THE "FLIGHTFURY."

"AWESOME SAUCE!" Antonio shouted extremely loudly.

"Whoa!!!" Jayden said sticking his hands on his cheeks "Is th...that re...re...really the FLIGHTFURY?"

"Yep, that is the FLIGHTFURY!" the pilot said.

They went to their plane.

The pilot said, "Please board the helicopter. I will be there shortly."

Both of them rushed to the helicopter without wasting any time. The pilot didn't take very long either. Finally, the time came for them to take off. They couldn't ever have imagined that they would actually get to fly in the sky in a helicopter.

The pilot started the engine and presto, they began their journey.

Antonio took out his phone and Jayden took out his novel, *The Hidden treasure in the Isle of Roha.*

Ben asked him, "Hey, Jayden. What are you reading?"

"Oh, this? This book is called *The Hidden Treasure in the Isle of Roha.*"

Antonio saw them talking and started taking pictures from above.

Jayden noticed him and said, "Dude! Are you disobeying what mom told you?"

But Antonio unexpectedly answered, "No."

"Dude, do you know what you have done?" Jayden said.

"No, what I have done?" Antonio asked him, worrying about what he had done.

"I'll tell you as soon as I know it," Jayden said. "But I guess it could lead us to something bad, I…" he continued telling him off when Ben interrupted them, "Boys you aren't getting into any trouble, are you?"

"What? No!" Antonio said.

"Unless we want to get in trouble, we won't get into trouble. And Ben please mind your own business!" Jayden said. He said all of this without looking at Ben.

"Why do you keep looking at me like that?" Antonio asked. "Because I thought that being an elder brother, it's your duty to share your things with me," Jayden replied.

"Nah, I don't think so," Antonio said.

"You're a bad brother. And know that I could totally bust you in front of mom. You wouldn't want that. Can a bad brother save you from mom? Well, I don't think so!" Jayden shouted at him.

After a few minutes, Jayden got tired of reading the novel.

He exclaimed, "This novel is so BORING!"

He stopped for a moment and saw Antonio taking pictures on the mobile.

He thought of asking him to share his...oh, not his phone, mom's phone with him. However, he knew that Antonio would not share the phone with him, so he didn't bother asking. Instead, he lay down to sleep for a bit. His leg slipped under the pilot's seat. When he was about to sleep, Ben shouted, "Hey, kids. Look down there, near the mountains."

"Whoa!!!" Antonio shouted.

"What? What happened?" Jayden asked as he tried to move towards Antonio's side but his leg was stuck under the pilot's seat. He pulled his leg from under the seat with some difficulty and felt as if he had pulled out something like a wire, or three to four wires. He looked down to check. He couldn't see clearly so he ignored it.

"Look down there. Can you see it?" Antonio pointed towards the mountains.

"No, it is probably too late, I will see it next time it shows up," Jayden said sadly.

"Jayden, now. There they are!" Antonio said to him. Jayden rushed to Antonio's side but he could not see anything below, when suddenly, Antonio said, "Hah! Fooled ya!"

"Ha! Ha! Very funny!" Jayden shouted at him.

But Antonio was still laughing.

"Excuse me, the snow is falling. How much time will it take us to reach there?" Ben asked Mr. William.

"Not much. 45 minutes at most at the current speed."

Jayden and Antonio were asleep.

"Maybe we should go higher as the snow is falling," the pilot said.

He tried to press down on the clutch but nothing happened. He tried again and again but it was stuck. The pilot feared that it could be extremely dangerous if the clutch was stuck. The pilot was in extreme stress.

"Is everything all right Mr. William? It seems that you are under extreme pressure."

William didn't want them to panic so he told Ben that everything was under control. Suddenly, Ben said, "William, shouldn't we be flying over Nunavut?"

As soon as he said this, they heard a strange noise.

BEEP! BEEP! BEEP!

"What's that awful noise?" Jayden cried.

"I thought it was you trying to wake me up from sleep," Antonio murmured.

"What is it, William? What is that sound? Is it some kind of warning?" Ben asked.

"Yes! It is a warning," William shouted.

"Of what?" Ben asked.

"The fuel is running low," William said to him.

"What should we do now?" Ben asked with an expression of fear on his face.

"I think we need to land," William said.

"In this extremely cold region, this could be very dangerous," Ben said.

"Whoa…whoa, slow down bud. What could be so dangerous? What are both of you talking about?" Antonio asked.

They began to whisper, "Should we tell them?" Ben asked.

"If you don't want to cause any more trouble, you should," William said.

He started shouting on the speaker, "MAYDAY! MAYDAY! MAYDAY!"

"What happened?"

"We need to do an emergency landing because we are almost out of fuel. And after we land, we are going ask for help through this speaker," Ben explained to them.

"What? Are you crazy? You don't even know if there is land underneath. There could be water!" Jayden shouted at them.

"That's a risk we need to take," Antonio said.

Suddenly, the sound became even louder. William checked for the cause and said, "The system...the tail rotor has caught fire."

He said, "Yeah, we found that out a second ago."

"Oh! Nothing new then," William said.

"Are there any parachutes?" Jayden asked.

"Parachutes? Yes! Antonio, check on the left, in the back. Can you see it?" William asked.

Antonio saw the box and opened it, but he found that there were only two parachutes there.

"What should do we now? Only two persons can land safely. What about the other two?" Jayden said.

Suddenly, William said, "Quickly, the helicopter is just 150 feet above the ground. It's not much longer until the helicopter crashes. We have to act quickly," William said.

But it turned out that his calculations were wrong. They were only left with fifteen minutes before they crashed.

"Jayden, Antonio…quick…wear the parachutes and jump. You go directly to the south. There's a city with a port. Go to the port and tell them to fly Jayden and you to Iqualit," Ben said.

"What about you? You'll die, Ben. We can't just leave Mr. William and you in this helicopter," Antonio said with a fearful expression on his face.

"Yeah! There has to be a way so that all of us can survive this," Jayden said.

"Mr. Ben is right. There's no way that all of us can survive. Quickly! You need to jump now and save your life," William said.

Both of them were very disappointed but they knew they had to jump. However, Antonio made Ben promise that no matter what Ben needed to survive.

"Just think about mom, Ben. I can't imagine what would happen to her if you died," he said hurriedly before jumping.

When he landed, he found that Jayden was

already there, looking in the direction of the helicopter. By the time Antonio came out of his parachute, he heard Jayden shouting, "NO!"

He looked in the direction of the helicopter. It wasn't burning!

Both of them were confused but soon the wind started blowing, and the snow started to fall. They had to think about how they would survive the night.

"What should we do now, Antonio? We can't survive an entire night in this kind of weather. We have to figure out a way soon," Jayden said.

Antonio looked around, rubbing his hands to warm them. He couldn't see anything except snow and the parachutes in which they had landed.

Suddenly, an idea came to his mind.

He said, "Get inside the parachute, quickly!"

Without wasting any time, both of them went under the parachutes, turning them into tents.

Chapter 7

GET… SET… SURVIVE

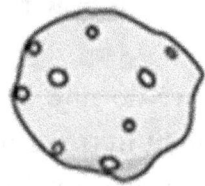

The next morning, Jayden yawned and turned around to wake Antonio up.

"Good morning Antonio, wake up," he said.

Surprisingly Antonio was not inside the parachute. Jayden walked out of the parachute and saw Antonio looking up in the direction in which they had last seen the helicopter at night.

"Antonio," Jayden said in a low tone.

"Oh! You're up already, morning Jayden," Antonio said.

"Yeah, what time is it?" Jayden asked him.

"It's 11'o clock right now."

"Whoa…I was sleeping for a really long time," Jayden said.

"What time did you get up?" he asked.

"Oh, just half an hour ago before you woke," Antonio said.

"Well, after what happened last night, what should we do now?" Jayden asked.

"Yeah, I think I know what we should do. We need to head in the direction we saw the helicopter falling. We need to find out where the helicopter crashed last night, but first, we need to look for a pond or something. I have to quench my thirst," Antonio said.

"What...seriously? Antonio, have you lost your mind? How are you are going to search for them in this kind of place? This place...Antonio... it never ends, and besides we are not even sure where to go and look for them," Jayden yelled at him.

"And besides, Ben told us to head south—"

"I DON'T CARE WHAT BEN SAYS. ALL I KNOW IS WE ARE GOING TO THE HELICOPTER CRASH SITE," Antonio yelled at him.

"Okay, fine. We'll go then," Jayden said.

"Jayden, I'm sorry. I didn't mean to yell at you like that. It's just that Ben makes mom happy and if anything happens to him like it happened to our father, it will break mom," Antonio explained.

"Okay, Antonio. Let's do it your way and find some water."

They started walking in the other direction and/kept on going and kept on going but didn't find any lake or pond.

Antonio saw something and said, "Jayden, look there. Do you see it?"

"Yeah," he replied. They both ran towards the shimmering blue.

"Well, we finally got water. Now drink it as fast as you can. I have a bad feeling about what might have happened to Ben and the pilot," Jayden said.

"Yikes! Think positive and do positive, besides nothing would have happe…"

Antonio suddenly stopped. He had a vision again. He saw that they were in a cave. Jayden's right leg was injured and there was a stranger with them as well.

"Antonio…Antonio…hello are you there?" Jayden was shouting in his ears. He suddenly came back to reality. His vision cleared as he heard a strange kind of noise.

Jayden asked, "Whoa! Dude what happened there? Where were you lost? And what were you saying?"

"Nothing happened. I was just lost for a moment. I was saying yeah, besides nothing would have happen…"

BOOM! The loud sound came from the direction where they thought the helicopter had crashed the other day. While they were looking in the opposite direction, a huge animal with a very large horn came wildly towards them from underwater.

"Ahh…" Jayden screamed, but suddenly something or someone pulled them. Antonio turned around to see who had saved them. They saw an old man with a large stick. He looked like a beggar or something.

"Who are you? And what was that?" Antonio asked.

"My name is Stephen James and that, my friend, was a Narwhal. It's an aquatic animal from the North Pole. Its tusk can grow 9 feet and it can weigh up to 22 pounds. They are natural predators like killer whales, polar bears and walruses. Your brother, is he dead?"

"I am Antonio and this is my younger brother, Jayden.

We came here because of a helicopter crash. And no, he is just unconscious," Antonio said.

"Well it was nice to meet ya! And I guess my job here is done. So, farewell, new guest."

As he was leaving, he turned around and said, "And yes, welcome to hell."

Antonio was struck by what the man said and started thinking about what he meant by 'Welcome to hell'.

"Uh huh…" Jayden came back to consciousness.

"What happened Antonio? Who was that man? What were both of you talking about?"

"He said his name was Stephen James. He looked like a beggar but he was as knowledgeable as a scientist."

"Well, he's gone now. We should probably head towards the helicopter before it gets dark."

After hours of travelling, it started snowing quite heavily. A snowstorm was fast approaching.

Jayden said, "We should stay put. The storm is getting worse. We should find some shelter."

They found a cave and decided to stay there until the storm had passed.

Chapter 8

BEN AND WILLIAM
MAKE IT ALIVE

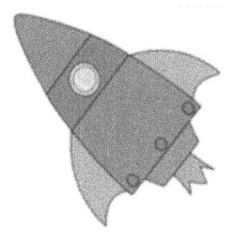

While, at the crash site, William and Ben were coming to terms with what had happened.

"Uh-huh...what ...what happened?" Ben squeaked.

"Oh, good god gracious, Ben! You're alive. There's a storm. Thanks to the snow, it kept the helicopter from burning. You were unconscious all the time," William explained.

"Any sign of Jayden and Antonio?" Ben asked.

"No. Not yet," William replied.

"We have to go and find them. Now!" Ben

said, even though he was wracked with pain.

"No, no. Ben, you're hurt because of the rod. You can barely walk. You can't act immediately. You need to rest. We'll go search for them in the morning. All right?" William said.

"Alright, we'll go search for them in the morning. Until then, can you find the first aid box?" Ben said.

"Okay, I'll go search for the first aid box. You stay right here."

Chapter 9

MAXIMUS: THE POLAR BEAR PET

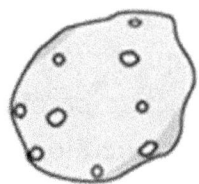

In Iqualit, the navigation room at the heliport was filled with urgency.

"Come over here, sir. It's an emergency," a man said. The supervisor ran inside the heliport and went over to a man sitting in the chair, "Sir, it's an emergency," he said.

He asked, "What happened?"

The man said, "We have lost the FLIGHT FURY'S signal. We can't track it, and it is not responding to our questions."

The navigation man said, "Should we inform the press?"

"Not now. We will let them know if we have absolutely no choice," he replied.

✿ ✿ ✿

In the morning, Ben woke and saw William stitching the wound he had received because of the rod.

"Almost done. It should be healed in a week or two," William said to him.

"Where did you learn to stitch?" Ben asked while trying to sit up.

"I took classes before becoming a pilot," said William, "I always wanted to become a doctor."

"Then why did you not become one?" Ben asked.

"My father was a pilot for 20-30 years. My sister was only 29 when she got married. Time passed, my sister was happy with her husband. My father got old and retired. One day, my father had a heart attack. We took him to the hospital. After half an hour, the doctor came from the operation theater. He shook his head and said that my father's heart rate was very slow. He said that my father had advanced cancer and he had only a week to live. I went inside my father's room. He was conscious again. My father told me that his last wish was that I become a pilot. I promised him that I would become a pilot and finally, after 5 years of work, I took an exam. I passed it. We were trained and I became a pilot..." William explained.

"Well that is a very touching story. Besides that, any sign of the boys?" Ben asked.

"No, not yet," William told him.

"Maybe we should head out to look for them," Ben said.

"Maybe...but your cut is not that small. You should rest here. I'll go and search for them," William said.

"No, it is going to be fine. Besides, it is just a cut. Come on," Ben said.

"I'll go with that but I am not sure about it."

✿ ✿ ✿

At the cave, where Jayden and Antonio had spent the night, Jayden woke up yawning.

"Morning, Antonio," Jayden said.

"Antonio, Antonio!" Jayden didn't see any sign of him in the cave.

He went outside to search for him. When he stepped out of the cave, all he could see were fir trees.

He looked for Antonio for half an hour but he couldn't find him anywhere. He went towards the cave believing that Antonio would return on his own.

As he reached the cave, he was scared half to death when he saw a polar bear inside the cave.

He was about to run away from there as fast as possible but he heard the polar bear growling in pain. When he took a few steps closer, he saw that the bear's leg was seriously injured.

He went closer to the bear to see if there was any way he could help him.

As he went closer, he stepped on a twig and the bear was alerted to his presence and growled at him angrily. Jayden was very scared. He put his paw forward to try and calm the bear. He wanted to make him understand that he would help him. The bear saw Jayden's hand and sat down sadly. Jayden went closer and the bear didn't try to attack him. He went near the bear to check his foot. He tore a part of his muffler and tied it on the bear's foot.

The bear tried standing up on his foot and, voilà, he stood up perfectly. He started licking Jayden's face.

When Antonio reached the cave with some fruits in his hand and saw the polar bear near Jayden, he shouted "Jayden get outta there!"

The bear jumped in front of Antonio, growling at him angrily. Jayden came in front of the bear to calm him.

After that, the polar bear calmed down. Jayden explained the whole situation to Antonio.

Antonio said, "Keeping him around wouldn't be a good idea. He is an animal. Who knows what he will do to us if gets hungry?"

"But he could also protect us from other wild animals," Jayden said, "Whatever, I am keeping him."

Jayden went outside the cave where the bear was sitting.

"Hey, Maximus! Come on bud, let's go," Jayden said.

"Seriously? 'Maximus'? That's the best you can do?" Antonio complained.

"What? Maximus is a good name. The bear likes it as well. Don't you, boy? Don't you?" Jayden asked.

"Whatever!" Antonio said and started walking the other way.

Suddenly, Antonio had another vision.

He saw that both of them were hidden behind a rock. He saw Maximus fighting a ferocious snow leopard.

"Whoa!" he squeaked.

"What happened, Antonio?"

"Huh! Nothing, nothing…just got a little cold," Antonio said.

"That didn't seem like nothing. He must be hiding something," Jayden thought.

Chapter 10

SARA KNOWS

While in Iqualit,

Sara had just come back home from the gro-
cery shop and was thinking of making a
phone call to Ben.

When she called his phone, she discovered that
Ben's phone was switched off. She thought that
Ben and the boys must be enjoying the trip, so she
decided to call later. She turned on the TV and was
shocked to see the news. Every news channel was
flashing the same headlines, 'A helicopter, 'Flight
Fury', location unknown, air forces are searching
everywhere around their last known location,
Annoatok.'

She had a strange feeling in the pit of her
stomach.

The next day in the morning, she tried to call uncle John. When uncle John picked up the phone, Sara asked him if she could talk to Jayden and Antonio. The boys' grandfather took the phone from uncle John and remarked, "We are very worried as well. Where are the boys? They haven't reached here!"

"What are you saying?" Sara asked, panicking.

"They left home three days ago."

"I don't know, Sara. The only thing I know is that they are not here. Please ring us if you hear anything about them," uncle John said and hung up the phone.

Sara was in tears after listening to what uncle John had just said. She didn't know what to do, whom to call. She needed to find Ben and her two boys.

Chapter 11

THE VAMPIRE

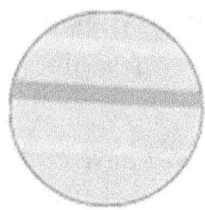

At the heliport, the men were carrying on a serious conversation.

"I hope telling the press about this was a good idea," the man thought to himself.

"Sir, the air force patrol hasn't gotten any useful information from there, and we still haven't been able to track them," the navigation guy said.

"Who were the passengers in that helicopter and who was the pilot?" the man asked.

"There was one adult, Ben Lake, and two children, Antonio James and Jayden James. The pilot was William Starc."

The man standing next to him asked, "What should we do now sir?"

"I…I don't know," the man said, looking disappointed.

✡ ✡ ✡

Elsewhere, Ben and William had set out in search of Antonio and Jayden.

"Ben, I think we should really relax for some time. We have been walking continuously for two-three hours. I can't walk anymore," William told him.

"No, William. We have to keep walking until we find my kids," Ben replied.

"We really need to rest for some time, otherwise we will lose our energy and we won't be able to continue further."

Finally, Ben had to agree with him and they stopped to rest for a while.

"Why don't your kids like you?" William asked.

"Actually, I am not their father," Ben replied.

"What?" William asked, "What do you mean you are not their father?"

"I am their step-father," Ben said, "And the only reason they stay with me is because I keep their mother happy."

Ben continued, "You know what, I think you were right. I really needed a break. My legs feel much more relaxed."

✡ ✡ ✡

Antonio and Jayden continued searching for the missing helicopter.
Jayden was getting very suspicious that Antonio was lying or hiding something from him. He pulled Antonio back to ask him what he was hiding from him but Antonio just wouldn't tell him. Jayden requested Antonio to tell him about what was happening to him. Maybe he could help but Antonio replied that he wasn't hiding anything and even if there was a problem he could handle it by himself.

Suddenly, out of nowhere, they heard sounds coming from the sky. The sounds were coming from helicopter wings. There were five helicopters. Both of them got very excited and started shouting for HELP at the top of their voices. Unfortunately, their voices were not heard.

The helicopters belonged to the most wanted villainous organization that operated in three different cities – Iqualit, Nuuk, and Annoatok

In the organization's helicopter, a strange conversation was going on.

"Sir, are you sure that The Hidden Place of Sacred Stones is here?" a soldier from the gang asked the leader who had an emerald stone right in the center of his armor. It shined like a diamond.

"Yeah, I am sure of it. My father, grandfather, great grandfather and all of my ancestors died searching for The Hidden Place of Sacred Stones. I am the only one left in my family who can find it because I am the only one who has succeeded in getting a map," said the leader, Satan Lucifer.

"Sire, won't the (HOE) HOLDERS OF EARTH try to stop our plan to find the hidden place," asked a soldier.

"No, I don't think they will interfere because I have someone from their agency working with me. Without his orders no one can do anything. Even if they try to stop us, we will be ready for them because we are not just a gang. We will be the richest gang in the whole galaxy. We will be more powerful than anything or anyone. Even (HOE) HOLDERS OF EARTH will be afraid of us. This is THE VAMPIRE and I am your leader, Satan Lucifer the destroyer."

"Hail Satan Lucifer, hail Satan Lucifer, hail Satan Lucifer," cheered the soldiers.

Ben and William decided to return to their search.

"I think we should get going now. Beside we have had a lot of rest," Ben said.

"Okay, let's go," William agreed.

Chapter 12

SARA DISCOVERS THE HELICOPTER CHANGE

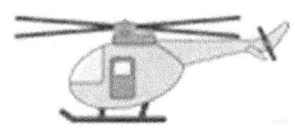

In Iqualit,

Leaving all her work Sara rushed to the heliport's main control system. She yelled at them, "Please find the launch details of the thunder ranger from 21ˢᵗ April."

As she said this, the controller quickly looked up the details, "Madam, are you sure there was a flight on 21ˢᵗ April of the thunder ranger?" the controller asked.

"There must be some mistake. There were only five flights that day—

1. SONIC MACHINE
2. BRIGHT STAR
3. FLIGHT FURY

4. HAILMAIN

5. BURNING SUN

"What!" she yelled at him, "That is impossible! How can there be no flight of the THUNDER RANGER?"

She went outside the cabin and suddenly, she thought of something. She ran back to the control room and asked the controller to tell her the names of the passengers who were in the helicopters. The controller did what she asked.

The details were listed under the following headings—helicopter name, passenger names—with the adult's name first, followed by the names of children/teenagers accompanying them.

Sonic machine,	Laurel & Quentin-None
Bright star,	Scott & lyla-Ben Jr.
Flight fury,	Ben-Antonio & Jayden
Hailmain,	James -None
Burning sun,	Oliver & felicity William

"Yes! Kane, put the list of names for the flight fury on the screen," Sara said.

"The adult passenger was Ben and the children accompanying him were Antonio and Jayden," Kane said.

"Did the flight fury's pilot return?" Sara asked.

"No, unfortunately, that helicopter never reached nuuk," he said.

"Come on, Kane. You're kidding? Tell me the pilot returned?" Sara ordered.

"You don't believe me?" Kane asked.

"No, it can't be true!" she replied.

"Come and have a look for yourself," Kane said.

FLIGHT DATE: 18 APRIL
PASSENGERS: ADULT 1- BEN LAKE
CHILDREN: 2-ANTONIO SMITH,
                       JAYDEN SMITH
RETURNED DATE: NOT CONFIRMED

"OH NO!" Sara squeaked.

Chapter 13

SURVIVE IN A CAVE
WITH A STRANGER

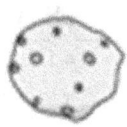

Disappointed, Antonio and Jayden kept going north. Both of them came up with the ideaof sitting on Maximus and telling him where to go. He would take them wherever they wanted to go.

The night was cold, and lighting struck the ground with great force. It was snowing very heavily.

"Jayden, tell Maximus to go into the bushes. I think I see something. I think I can see fire," Antonio told Jayden.

"I can see it too," Jayden said. "Come bud, head towards that light."

Maximus ran towards the light.

When they went closer, they discovered a cave. When they reached the opening of the cave, they went inside cautiously. As soon as they entered, they found a man in the cave. The man became aware of their presence and out of nowhere, he pulled out a gun and pointed it at them. However, it didn't take them long to recognize each other.

"You two boys again! Look, there's an animal behind you!" he exclaimed, exasperated.

"No, no. That's my pet. Don't shoot!" Jayden shouted.

"Stephen! You?" Antonio said.

"You know that guy?" Jayden asked him.

"Yeah. This is the guy who saved us from the narwhal," Antonio told Jayden.

"Narwhal?"

"Oof, remember when we found a lake and suddenly an aquatic animal came out of the water. It was a narwhal. He saved our lives but you were unconscious," Antonio said.

"Now coming to the point WHY ON EARTH DO YOU HAVE A GUN?"

"I don't need to tell you, kid," Stephen said.

"Yes, you do. Why do you have a gun? Where did you find it?" Antonio asked him.

"Look, I know you want to stay here until morning. I am gonna allow you to stay only on one condition. You can't ask any questions about anything you see. So, do we have a deal?" Stephen asked them.

"No, we're not gonna stay with a total stranger, especially one with a gun," Antonio told him.

"Fine, kid. The cave's exit is right there. Go if you want and come back any time. I'll welcome you," Stephen said.

"Fine. Come on, Jayden!" Antonio ordered.

"What? I am fine with the deal. I am staying. We barely survived half an hour out there without shelter. And now, the weather is more dangerous than ever. We won't even survive a minute out there, brother," Jayden told Antonio.

"Anyway, there is no way I am going to stay here," Antonio said.

He climbed onto Maximus and told him to move, but Maximus wouldn't move an inch.

"Maximus, put him down," Jayden said. And Maximus threw him down.

"Ooouch, that hurts," Antonio cried.

"If you still don't want to stay here, I can't stop you," Jayden said.

"Fine, I'll stay, but only for one night," Antonio said.

"Okay and thanks," Jayden replied.

The next morning, Antonio woke up to find Jayden gone.

"Aah..." Antonio woke up with a yawn, "Good morning Jayden...Jayden...JAYDEN. Oh no, Maximus. Where did he go...? Stephen?" Antonio shouted. When he turned around, Stephen wasn't there either.

"Where are these guys???" Antonio thought to himself as he came out of the cave.

The moment he stepped out of the cave he saw them coming towards the cave chatting with each other.

"Hey guys, over here!!!" Antonio shouted.

"Told you he would get up before we returned to the cave," Jayden whispered to Stephen.

"Yeah, I am coming, Antonio."

"Where'd you guys go? I was scared," Antonio said.

"Come on scaredy cat, we just went fishing. See? Maximus and I caught fish in this bucket and Stephen caught fish in that bucket. Maximus and I caught more fish than Stephen," Jayden said.

"Hey, you had an animal. That's cheating," Stephen remarked.

"That wasn't cheating. That was an advantage and besides, you had a fishing rod, so how is that not cheating?" Jayden said.

"Wait, what? Di...did you just say that he has a fishing rod?" Antonio asked Jayden. "Oh, yeah.

He just picked up a few things from the ground, and did something with them, and voilà, it became a fishing rod. Isn't that interesting?" Jayden said.

"The fish is cooking. Come on, let's eat," Stephen said.

"Already on my way," Jayden said.

"Come on, Jayden. I think we should get going now," Antonio said.

"What? No, not now. Can't you see I am eating? You should try some too. It is really good," Jayden said. "Fine, then. Eat quickly. We don't have much time to waste," Antonio said.

"So, how did you get here in the first place?" Stephen asked.

"We were heading to our uncle & aunt's house when our helicopter crashed. We don't exactly know what happened but the handle wasn't rotating in any direction. There were only two parachutes in the helicopter. Ben told us to wear them and to head south towards a city called nuuk when we landed. Ben said it would be the first city we would reach. My uncle and aunt also live in that city. He told us to go to the port and tell them to give us a ride to Iqualit and my mom would pay them," Jayden explained.

"So, who is this 'Ben' in your story?" asked Stephen.

"Ben is our step-father. Our father died a year ago in a car accident and our mom married Ben. But we never refer to him as our father or even step-father," Antonio told him.

"You know, my father died 32 years ago and just like you I hated my step-dad very much. But one day, my mom walked into my room and she found me crying. She said those who are gone are gone, they never come back but we can always make new relationships. Although, step-fathers can't take your dad's place, they can love you as much as your real father did. Since then, I have always seen my real dad in my step-father," Stephen said.

"Oh, tha…that's nice," Jayden said.

"But how did you end up here? A helicopter crash?"

"I didn't end up here, I was sent here," Stephen said.

"What, you were sent here? Who sent you?" Jayden asked curiously. He wanted to know what had gotten Stephen there.

"Jayden, I think we should get going now. We won't have to travel too far, I think. We are quite close, I feel," Antonio said.

"No, I won't go until he tells us why he was sent here and by whom," Jayden told him.

"Your brother is right. You should go, I wish you good luck," Stephen said.

"No, Stephen. Please tell us," Jayden said

"You don't need to know, kid," Stephen said to him.

"Maybe we could help in some way."

"GO!" Stephen yelled at him. His yelling caught Maximus' attention. Maximus came running towards him to save Jayden from being hurt. But Jayden came in front of Maximus to stop him.

"Fine, we'll go then," Jayden said.

Saying this, they both headed out of the cave.

Chapter 14

SATAN LUCIFER

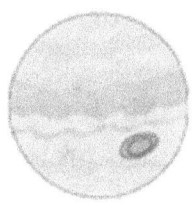

"Come on, get the woods out. We don't have much time," said Satan Lucifer.

"My lord, we're here. So how will we find the hidden place?" asked Satan Lucifer's assistant, Zaebos. "'We'? Oh no, they are going to find the hidden place."

As soon as Satan Lucifer uttered those words, two soldiers appeared on the scene. They were leading five people out of a helicopter.

"My lord, who are they?" Zaebos asked.

"They are archeologists. I kidnapped them from New York to help us find the hidden place," replied Satan Lucifer

"How will they help us, sire? Can't we use our men to find the hidden place?" Zaebos asked.

"Yes, we have our men to find the hidden place but they are not well trained. I have not kidnapped these archeologists without thinking. They are some of the most famous archeologists from all over the world," Satan Lucifer explained.

"I don't know how they will help us. Yet. Bring out the archeologists," Satan Lucifer told the soldiers. He then ordered the soldiers to make the archeologists kneel before him. After the archeologists kneeled in front of him, he reached out for man from their group and put a sword near his throat and said, "If you don't answer my questions in ten seconds I will chop of his head—

How do you find places which are underneath the lands?"

One them stood up and said, "The places beneath the lands are very fertile and so soft that one wrong step, and the whole surface can break into pieces."

Satan Lucifer then asked another question—

How would you know that there's a place under this land?"

Another man stood up and squeaked, "There is something called a frequent quantity gadget. We can use it to check if there is a hidden city underneath the land."

Satan Lucifer continued asking the archeologist questions—

How will that gadget help you tell me?

The man said, "If we are standing on land under which there is a city underneath, the arrow on the gadget will point towards the red mark. If we are near such a place, it will point towards the yellow mark. If we are far from such land, the gadget will point towards the green point."

Satan Lucifer took the sword away from his neck and roughly pushed him towards the group.

"Pack the stuff you need. You are going for a field trip tomorrow. Take them away and lock them up," ordered Satan Lucifer.

"Sire, what if they try to run away?" Asked Zaebos.

"I know they will try to run away. This is why I am sending five soldiers with them. You will also accompany them. Make sure the guard is well armed," said Satan Lucifer.

Ben and William happened to be crossing the gang's hiding place just then and heard everything. They had hidden themselves about half a mile away behind a tree.

"Oh, NO, NO, NO, NO. This is bad. This is really, really bad. We have to help those archeologists," William whispered.

"Oh? How are we going to do that? They have an army. And we are just two guys," Ben said.

"But we have to do something! We can't just sit here," William said.

After that there was a moment of silence then suddenly Ben said, "Okay, I have an idea that might work. At night, when they will all be asleep, we will go into their hideout and find the archeologists. This way we only need to get past five guards and not the entire army. We will be able to free them this way. Alright?" Ben asked William.

"What? That idea only works in movies, and sometimes it doesn't. This won't work. Think of something else," William said.

"Fine, then. Let's hear your idea," Ben said.

"You know what? I have a better idea," William said.

"Great and what's that?" he asked.

"We…we…" William stuttered

"Yeah?" Ben said

"We…we go with your plan," William said.

"Finally, he is coming to his senses," squeaked Ben.

"But just so you know, it is not going to work," William said.

AT NIGHT…

"Psst…psst…" William whispered as Ben had fallen asleep.

"Uh-huh, what!" Ben murmured.

"I think we should go now," William said.

"Alright," Ben agreed.

They silently went into the vampire's hideout. They were both looking around when suddenly, Ben accidentally stepped on his shoelace. He went in through an open door to tie his shoelace. After he tied his shoelace and stood up, he looked around because he wasn't sure about his whereabouts. It was dark all around. There was not even a little light. He was heading out when he saw something which caught his attention. He went towards it. It was like a cage made out of very hard metal, sealed from the side. He saw a biometric lock on the front. It required a password. He tried to put his ear against it. Suddenly, he was sure he heard a very faint voice screaming. He knew he had to be sure that SOMEONE was inside it. But he couldn't say anything because someone might have heard him. At the same time, he heard William whispering his name outside. He ran outside the door. William saw him and ran towards Ben and said, "Don't get lost here."

"Okay," Ben whispered back.

They were both looking in different directions when Ben saw the archeologists locked up in a cage.

"Hey, there," Ben said very, very slowly to William.

They headed towards where the archeologists were locked up.

"Hey, psst...hey, wake up," William whispered to them.

Hearing his voice, one of the archeologists woke up. William was glad that he had woken up and said, "Hey, here, don't worry. My friend and I are here to help you."

The man got excited when he heard that. He woke up the others.

"Do you know where the keys are?" Ben asked.

"One of the soldiers has it. They are in that cabin," a girl said.

"Oh no! How will we get the keys now? Maybe we should just give up," saying this, Ben started heading the other way but William stopped him saying, "Wait, I am going inside the cabin to get the key."

"What! William, that is suicide. We should run away before we get caught," Ben shouted at him.

"There is no other way," William said. He gathered all his courage and went inside the cabin. He was trying to be very careful not to make even a single sound. He was even breathing very slowly. He looked around and saw a soldier's t-shirt and the keys hanging next to it. He went towards it. He slowly took the keys and ran outside the cabin.

"I got it. I got the keys," William whispered. Without wasting any time, William opened the lock.

The next day in the morning, they were all walking in a random direction, not knowing where to go.

"What should we do now?" William asked.

"I thought you would know because this was YOUR idea," Ben said.

"We haven't met each other properly, right?" asked a girl.

"No, besides now we can properly introduce ourselves. My name is William Stack and this is my friend Ben Lake," William told them.

"Well let's start with our introductions. My name is Gwen Carol. And these are my friends as well as partners- Steve Jones, Hunk Lincoln, Mary Roy and Tyler harper," Gwen said, while pointing to each person in the group.

"So why did you even help us?" asked Steve Quizzical.

"Well there are two reasons behind that. First, I thought after you've found the hidden place..." Mary interrupted William, saying, "How do you know about the hidden place?"

"Both of us heard your conversation with that man. We do not know him," Ben told her.

"How?" asked hunk.

"We...we were crossing from there and we saw their hideout. We saw you guys on your knees in front of that guy," replied William.

"Oh, now it makes sense," said Tylor.

"What are you guys doing here anyway?" asked Steve. "Both of us came here because of a helicopter crash," answered Ben.

"What happened?" Gwen asked.

"William and I..." Ben suddenly stopped.

"What, what happened?" Gwen asked.

She turned around and saw five soldiers coming from the opposite direction.

They came closer together and started running away from the soldiers. Unfortunately, five soldiers came towards them from that direction as well. They tried to run the other way but the soldiers were coming from every direction. They were surrounded.

Satan Lucifer walked towards them and went up to Ben and William.

He asked them, "Who are you?"

"We are the people who helped them escape from you, monster!" answered Ben.

"Well, you know, I hate people who call me monster. Let me tell you some good news. I am going to let you live because you are our new guest," Satan Lucifer said.

"So, you mean that you won't kill us?" asked William.

"Oh, I will kill you, just not yet. When I get bored of you, then I will kill you both. Lock 'em up soldiers," Satan Lucifer said.

"And trust me, at that point, you will beg me to kill you."

Chapter 15

THEY FOUND A PART OF THE HELICOPTER

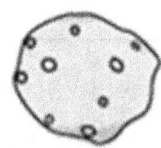

*M*eanwhile, *Antonio and Jayden had been walking for days. They were tired and hungry. They were nowhere closer to a city where they could ask for help.*

"Antonio, we've been traveling for days. This doesn't seem to end," Jayden said.

"Yes, I know Jayden. But we have no choice," Antonio told him.

"But I am hungry," Jayden said.

"Fine. We'll stop for a few minutes, and then we'll go and search for food. Alright?" said Antonio.

"Alright," replied Jayden.

They got down from Maximus's back to search for food. Antonio said to Jayden, "Go search for fruits in that direction and I will go the other way. But don't go too far, okay?"

"Alright," replied Jayden.

They both went in opposite directions. Jayden had no clue where he was going. He kept on walking, looking here and there for something to eat, when suddenly he saw some pears on the top of a tree. He tried several times to climb to the top of the tree, but he didn't succeed in any of his attempts. Suddenly, he had an idea. He decided to punch the tree just as he had seen in movies, where the hero punches the trees and fruits fall down from them. He tried the same thing but after he tried to punch the tree, he was sorry he had made the attempt.

"Ooouch! Aw man! It broke my knuckles," he cried painfully. He tried very hard to think but couldn't think of any ideas. In the end, for the last time he tried to climb the tree, and suddenly he realized that he wasn't falling. He was still holding a branch of the tree. With all his effort, he jumped onto another branch. Just by jumping from one branch to another, he reached the top of the tree.

"Ah, finally, I managed to reach the top. Let me just take some fruits," Jayden said. Just as he said that, he took off his hands from the branch he was using as support to prop himself up. This made him lose his balance and he fell from the tree with a big thump.

"Ouch!" he cried in pain. He tried to get up. He looked up and found himself staring into big red eyes. Suddenly, he heard a voice from behind.

"Jayden, Jayden!"

Jayden realized that it was Antonio calling him but when he turned around he saw that the red eyes had disappeared. Jayden ran back to their meeting place.

"Hey, I found some fruits to eat. Did you have any luck?" Jayden asked.

"None, but I did find something that we have been looking for," Antonio said.

"Huh, like you found the helicopter?" Jayden murmured.

"Yeah. I did," Antonio said.

"What?" Jayden said.

Antonio turned around and started walking towards the woods. Jayden followed him. After walking through some itchy bushes, he saw something he hadn't expected to see ever again. He saw some parts of the helicopter.

"The thing that we were searching for three days...*three days*...Antonio, and all of a suddenly we found it," Jayden said with an expression of victory on his face.

"We surely did, but we didn't find what we were really searching for," Antonio told him.

"What do you mean?" Jayden asked him, confused.

"I mean Ben and William…they are not here," Antonio said.

"Oh man! I mean that's good news. Isn't it?" Jayden said.

"Well, I am not sure about that. I mean it would be good to know whether they are alive or if they were able to get away from here," Antonio replied.

"Who knows? Maybe someone took them while they were unconscious or maybe moved their dead bodies elsewhere?" Jayden said.

"Ssh, Ssh think positive, and please hope that nothing happens to them," Antonio said.

"Oh god, you and your Ben," Jayden said.

They started searching the helicopter in case they found something useful there.

Suddenly, Jayden called Antonio and told him, "Hey! Look, I found Ben's mobile."

He opened the mobile to send a message to their mother. But he discovered the mobile's battery was almost dead. "Come on! Come on! Quickly, Jayden. Do it quickly," shouted Antonio.

"Phew! Done!" said Jayden.

"Done at last. Now, after mom reads this message, she will find a way to help us."

"Nice, good job," said Antonio.

Jayden said thanks to him.

"Oh no!" muttered Antonio.

"What, what happened?" asked Jayden.

Antonio pointed to Ben's blood which had spilled when he had gotten hurt. Antonio went closer to it and touched it.

"What are you doing?" asked Jayden.

"I was checking if the blood has dried. It doesn't seem fresh," Antonio said, "I think Ben and William left days ago, if they survived the crash," Jayden said.

"Well, that is good to hear. But what do we do now?"

"I...don't know," Antonio said.

Chapter 16

THE ARCHEOLOGIST
FIGURE OUT THE PLAN

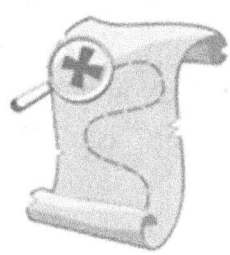

Ben and William were put in a different lock-up than the archeologists.

"Hey, guard! Why can't you keep all of us in the same lock-up? It's not like we are going to run away again with all this tight security again," asked William.

"Shut up," the soldier replied.

"Wow! Shut up. That's a really good answer, isn't it Ben?" William said.

"William, seriously...just shut up," Ben told him.

"Fine...I'll just sit here. You don't care," William said.

"Trust me, I won't," Ben replied.

At Satan Lucifer's operation base, preparations were underway for the search for the hidden city.

As soon as they entered Satan Lucifer's base, they saw hundreds of men building a giant container.

When the archeologists saw the container... they were shocked as if they had seen something more terrible and terrifying than a ghost.

"Huh! That's funny. You guys are building a washing machine. Are you staying here for another 10 years or something?" asked William.

"Someone make this Shute bag shut up or I am going to chop off his head," the soldier shouted.

"Whoa! Calm down...there is no need for that...besides, your boss wouldn't want that," Ben said to the soldier.

"Oh, don't you worry. There won't be any trouble if any of my soldiers kill you," Satan Lucifer said from behind.

"What! You said you wouldn't kill us," William said.

"Yet..." Satan Lucifer said to them.

"We met each other like 4 hours ago and you are already bored of us," Ben said.

"But you are not very important to me either," Satan Lucifer told him.

Ben didn't want to take the conversation any further so he didn't reply.

The soldier threw them back into the lock-up.

"Hey, do you have to do that all the time?" William asked.

"What? I like to do it. It makes me feel strong," the soldier said.

"Whatever," Ben muttered.

In their lock-up, the archeologists were discussing about the giant cylinder that was being built.

"Oh, no! This is bad, very bad," said hunk.

"Hey, would you mind? You're speaking too loudly," interrupted William.

"Sorry," replied Mary.

"What are you discussing?" William asked.

"We—" Gwen said when she was interrupted by Stephen, "What are you doing? They don't know anything, and besides I don't trust them. Especially the other one."

"You don't trust them but I do. They helped us escape. How can you not trust them after what they have done for us?" Gwen asked Stephen.

Although Stephen felt exasperated, he agreed to tell Ben and William what they were discussing.

"The giant cylinder? It is an 'Indestructible Natural Power Dynamite'. It is something which is extremely devastating," Gwen told them.

"Huh, fancy name. What would Satan Lucifer want with that toy?" asked Ben.

"Excuse me, didn't she make it clear? It is a bomb, dynamite, not a toy," Ben told William.

"Once Satan Lucifer finds 'The Hidden Place of Sacred Stones', he will take all the treasure from there and blast the ground," whispered Tyler.

"But why? He will have all the gold he wants so why blast The Hidden Place of Sacred Stones?" asked Ben.

"For as long as I have heard about the hidden place, there have been rumors that are only a few people in the entire world can enter it. In recent times, though, the legend has changed. It is said that only one man on the entire planet, and we don't know this person's identity, can enter the hidden place and pass the guardians. It is said that he has been chosen by the guardians but the legends also say that only a man who has a heart filled with sweetness, kindness, politeness and has no evil thought can enter the 'Hidden Place'," explained Gwen.

"Okay. In that case, if only this one person can enter the hidden place, how will Satan Lucifer enter the hidden place even if he finds it?" asked William quizzically.

"Yeah, I think he is right, Gwen. Only one person can enter and I know there aren't a lot of people who have these qualities. Maybe there is something we don't know about the legend."

"I think the chosen one is here. I think that Satan Lucifer knew who was chosen by the guardians and he has somehow found a way to bring him here," said Ben.

"How do you know?" asked William

"Remember last night when I got lost?" Ben asked.

"Yeah," William said.

"I didn't actually get lost. I accidently went through a door and I found a cage. It was like this but large. It was made up of metal sealed from all sides. I heard a voice from inside. It sounded like someone who was in pain. There was a biometric lock on the cage and it required a password," Ben said.

"But are you sure it was him? I mean the chosen one?" Mary asked.

"No, but who would be inside a special prison? Why isn't he in regular lock-ups like these? Whoever it is, they are probably very important to Satan Lucifer," Ben said.

"Hey, Gwen. Even if they make the guy go through the guardians, how will they get in?" William asked.

"Well, according to the legends the person who has been chosen by the guardians is also the ruler of the guardians. Satan Lucifer knows this. The guardians turn to stone once their master is not in the middle line. They turn to stone because they have to make a protective barrier," Gwen explained when she was interrupted.

"There are only two guardians?" William asked with shock.

"Yes, two guardians who are capable of decreasing the world's population by half," Gwen said.

"Ooh," William muttered.

"As I was saying, I think they will force him to stand in between the guardians. As soon as this is done, they will go in," Gwen said.

"Won't the guardians stop them?" asked Ben.

"They can't. If they try to stop them, they will end up hurting their ruler," Hunk said.

"So, if their ruler is not standing in between them, the guardians can attack them?" asked William.

"No, that is what she said earlier. The moment their ruler steps out, the guardians will turn to stone in order to make a protective shield so no one can enter," explained Tyler.

"So, that was his plan all along?" Mary said with shock.

All of them quietened when they heard footsteps coming closer.

Two soldiers appeared in front of them. One of them came and opened the archeologist's lock-up.

"Come on, Satan Lucifer has ordered your presence," he said.

The archeologists went with him. When they reached the operation base, Satan Lucifer said, "Ah...my guests!"

"Well, I don't really think we're 'guests'," said hunk.

Satan Lucifer glanced at the soldier who was behind the archeologists, and the soldier put his sword against Hunk's back.

"Ah, and here we are...your 'peaceful' guests who don't need to be threatened," said hunk and laughed nervously.

"All of you are going tomorrow to look for the hidden place, and I will be sending my finest, strongest and fastest...." Satan Lucifer was saying when he was interrupted by Zaebos, "I think that's enough appreciation, my lord."

"All right, Zaebos." Satan Lucifer replied, "So, as I was saying, you will be accompanied by two of my soldiers. If any of you tries to run away my soldier will kill someone else from the group. Do you understand?"

"Yes, yes," all of them replied unanimously.

"Good. Soldier take them away and lock them up," Satan Lucifer ordered.

Chapter 17

THE INTERNATIONAL SUPREME GROUP OF VILLAINS (ISGV)

Antonio and Jayden looked at the remains of the helicopter, wondering what to do next.

"Let's go," Antonio said.

"Go, but where?" asked Jayden.

"We have to find both of them," Antonio said.

"Antonio are you mad? Is this a joke? First, you wanted to find the helicopter and now this? Antonio, we should be headed towards the nearest city," Jayden said.

"I don't know anything. We just need to find them. I will not go anywhere without them," Antonio said.

"Look, Antonio. I appreciate what you are doing, but this is craziness. This place is so big. Even if we try to look for them, we might not be able to find them even in a million years. We are not gonna find them. We will not be able to accomplish anything." Jayden explained.

But Antonio stood up and said, "Look as far as I know, it's been three days so they couldn't have gotten very far. If we start looking for them now, maybe we can find them."

"Ah…fine," Jayden said.

"But this is the last, do you hear me, last thing I am doing for your sake."

"Okay, thanks Jayden," Antonio replied.

"So…where should be begin?" asked Jayden.

"Um…we should start looking…that way," Antonio said, pointing towards the east side.

"You're just guessing, right?" Jayden said.

"Yeah, either way let's go, shall we?" said Antonio.

"Yes, let's go," Jayden replied.

They both climbed up on Maximus's back and Jayden told him to head east. Maximus started moving east. They kept walking and walking and walking for hours which made Jayden feel sleepy. He slept like he hadn't slept in days and Antonio slept on top of him, snoring like an elephant and drooling all over his shirt. Suddenly, Jayden felt something wet on his back and realized Antonio was drooling all over him. He yelled at him, "Antonio ew…it's disgusting."

Antonio returned to reality.

"Huh…What?" Antonio squeaked.

It took him a few minutes to realize that he had drooled all over Jayden's shirt.

"Oh…sorry about the drooling," he apologized to Jayden.

"Its fine," Jayden replied.

As he was speaking, he suddenly noticed some footprints in the snow. Jayden got off Maximus' back and he went closer to inspect the footprints.

"Hey, Antonio look at these footprints," Jayden said, "Don't they look like Ben or William's footprints?" Antonio asked.

"I don't think it's their footprints. Look, these footprints are different. They are oval shaped," explained Jayden.

"If these footprints don't belong to Ben or William, whose could they be?" asked Antonio.

"It could be anybody's. No, wait a minute," Jayden said.

He looked at Maximus and glanced at his paws. He realized they had been roaming around in circles all this time.

"NOOOOO, THIS CAN'T BEEEEE," Jayden shouted at the top of his voice. He screamed so loudly that a snow leopard heard his voice and ran towards them.

"You, you wretched person, it's all because of you. We have lost precious time. By now we could have been halfway to a city," Jayden told him angrily.

"Don't blame me. It's all because of that stupid bear of yours," Antonio said.

"Don't blame him for something that you have done. It was your idea to find Ben and William, and who knows maybe they are already on their way to the nearest city, thinking that we are headed that way as well," Jayden said, when suddenly the snow leopard attacked him from behind and scratched Jayden with his nails. Jayden fell forward and his head hit a tree. He fainted immediately.

Antonio shouted loudly, "JAYDEN!"

The snow leopard jumped at him too but Maximus punched him on the side of his face while the leopard tried to attack him.

While Maximus distracted the leopard, Antonio dragged Jayden out of the way behind a large rock. He started crying and said, "Jayden please wake up, Jayden wake up. I admit it was my mistake. Please, Jayden, please wake up."

But Jayden didn't move even a little bit. He was still lying in Antonio's arms. He could see Maximus and the snow leopard fighting each other from behind the rock. They were punching, hitting and scratching each other with their nails. Suddenly, the snow leopard hit Maximus so hard that he fell to the ground. The snow leopard jumped to hit the final blow. Antonio closed his eyes as he couldn't see Maximus dying. As soon as he closed his eyes, he heard the sound of a gun. He slowly opened his eyes and saw the leopard lying on the ground. It was not moving anymore. Maximus was running towards them.

He could see Stephen standing in the distance but suddenly everything started to blur. He fell on the ground. His eyes closed as he fainted. After a while, he gained consciousness and opened his eyes. He realized that Jayden and he were on Maximus' back and Stephen was in front of Maximus. He fainted again.

After a few hours, Jayden woke up and found himself in a cave. Antonio was sitting near him, holding his hand. He could see an expression of extreme worry and concern on Antonio's face.

"What...huh, what happened, Antonio? Where are we?" he asked, confused.

"Jayden! Oh, good gracious, you are all right. I have been worried sick about you," Antonio said with relief.

"You're here in my cave and you're hurt. But you are fine now," Stephen said.

Jayden pulled up his t-shirt and saw bandages around his body.

"What happened?" he asked.

"A snow leopard attacked you from behind. You ran into a tree and fainted. Maximus fought the snow leopard," said Antonio.

"But how did we get here? With him..." Jayden looked at Stephen awkwardly.

"I don't know. I fainted too. The last thing I remember seeing were the two of us on Maximus, and Stephen was talking to him. I guess he was leading him here," Antonio explained.

"Here, drink this soup. You will heal faster," said Stephen.

"I won't drink it," replied Jayden.

"It will only help you," Stephen said.

"No," Jayden insisted.

"Fine. I am sorry," Stephen said. "For what?" asked Jayden?

Suddenly, Stephen hit Jayden on his neck with two of his fingers and Jayden's mouth automatically opened. Stephen fed him some of the soup.

"What are you doing to my brother?" Antonio asked.

Stephen didn't reply. He just punched Jayden's stomach lightly with his wrist. And Jayden automatically swallowed the soup. After this odd sequence of events, Jayden became normal.

"What did you do to me?" asked Jayden.

"The joint which allowes the head to turn from side to side is called the pivot joint. The side of the brain which is joined to the pivot joint is connected to your mouth. So, when I hit you on the neck with two of my fingers, your pivot joint reacted and your brain sent a signal to your mouth and you opened it. And when I hit your stomach with my wrist, the food pipe did the job and closed your mouth," Stephen explained.

"So, you're a zoologist and an anatomist?" asked Antonio.

"And a vet," Stephen added. "Ugh...achoo... achoo... achoo..." Jayden sneezed loudly.

"What did you put in that... soup?" he asked.

"A few drops of pain killer, a few mint leaves and a ball of snow," Stephen told him.

Hearing this, Jayden's expression changed, as if he was going to throw up.

"You..." Antonio said when Stephen interrupted him.

He whispered, "Ssh..."

"What happened?" asked Antonio.

"Someone's coming here," he said.

"Look at the shadows there."

"Oh, yes. I see it too," Jayden whispered.

Stephen slowly and silently took out his gun and stood up. He went there very slowly.

"What are you doing?" Antonio asked silently.

Without uttering a world, Stephen moved there and he pointed the gun at the people. Although, he was as fast as lightening, he was almost ambushed by six soldiers outside. He quickly shot two of them. While he was dealing with the soldiers, Antonio and Jayden hid behind the rock on which they had been sitting. One of the soldiers killed the other three soldiers. William was very confused. "Who are you?" he asked.

Then he slowly took off his mask and said, "It's me, William." Stephen gasped in shock. Then, the men hugged each other.

"You know this guy, Stephen?" Antonio asked, coming out from behind the rock.

Suddenly, the soldier shot a bullet in Antonio's direction. It barely missed him by half an inch.

"HOLY MOLY! What are you? A big idiot or a huge idiot, I think," Antonio shouted at him.

"All the idiots are the same," Jayden whispered.

"Oops! Sorry. My fault," the soldier apologized.

Antonio shouted, "Happy realization. I know it was your fault."

But the soldier continued, "Who are they, Stephen?" "Oh them, we keep running into each other," Stephen told him.

"Yeah, he looks like a soldier. What? Are you coming here from a battle or something?" Jayden asked.

"No, but there is going to be a battle," the soldier said.

"What? What are you talking about? Wait!" Stephen stopped all of a sudden and then he continued, "These soldier's uniforms seems familiar."

"Yes, they are," the soldier said.

"Does that mean he is here?" Stephen asked.

"Yes, Stephen he is here. And he is not alone. He has brought along an army to find the hidden world of sacred stones," the soldier said. "What is the hidden place of sacred stones?" Antonio asked, in a strange voice.

"Tell us from the beginning."

"It all started years ago..." Stephen said, "As early as the 16th century, many prominent people correctly believed that the North Pole was in a sea, which in the 19th century was called the Open Polar Sea. Several expeditions set out to find the way, generally with whaling ships, already commonly used in the cold northern latitudes. The expeditions were organized by an organization called (HOE) HOLDERS OF THE EARTH. Both of us belong to this organization. In 1909, when Robert Peary found the North Pole, this place, the hidden world, was a part of the North Pole, which was in the sea. After centuries, the sea level dropped and the North Pole came to the surface. All of this happened because of a gigantic and very dangerous earthquake. The hidden world sank into the Arctic Ocean, but every 10 years because of a tide reaction it appears again. Robert stayed here for a year and discovered the hidden world. He also discovered plutonium supernatural nucleus power stones but he was only able to take one of them with him. Before he died, he told a guy named Gerard Lucifer about the hidden city. He told him the location of the stones. Gerard found out about the power of the plutonium supernatural nucleus stones, and as time passed, he became obsessed with it. He needed more of the power, so he set sail to the North Pole. He doesn't know everything but since the stone was passed on to him, he is in possession of it."

"But how does he know when the city will appear? After a year has passed, it could surface any day?" Antonio asked.

"Yeah, they keep a record of everything. They know when it last it appeared, so they know it, as we do. It will appear seven days from today, I think."

"Who is "he" you are talking about?" Antonio asked. "Let's just name him You-Know-Who, even though we do not know who they are talking about," Jayden said.

"The Voldemort you're talking about, in this story, he is someone called Satan Lucifer," the soldier answered.

Antonio and Jayden's mouths fell open.

"What? You are not the only ones who have read the HARRY POTTER book series," the soldier said.

"SANTA LU-WHO, what was the name again?" Antonio asked.

"It's SATAN LUCIFER not SANTA LU-WHO. It spells S-A-T—" the soldier guy said.

"Ah-ta-ta-ta-ta, I know how to spell it. And I don't have time to learn it anyway," Antonio said.

"Fine, besides, he is the head of the International Supreme Group of Villains (ISGV). He came here to search for The Hidden Place of Sacred Stones.

Satan Lucifer has the strength of ten elephants," the soldier said.

"Hey, wait! I think I have heard of it," Antonio mumbled.

"What? How do you know about it?" William asked.

"Jayden, do you remember the night before dad died we went to his room. And do you remember what we found there?" Antonio asked.

"I'm not sure…there were a lot of papers lying around. I only remember a few of those papers," Jayden replied.

"No, not that. Remember you always wanted to sit on the chair which was covered with leopard skin…" Antonio said, trying to make him remember.

"Yeah, I remember. Antonio, you're a genius. I remember now. I sat down on it. I saw a file on Dad's desk. It was designed and maintained very well and it had a sign on it: IMPORTANT-DO NOT TOUCH. The sign was written on the front cover," Jayden said.

"So, what did you do?" the soldier asked.

"What do you think I did…?" Jayden chuckled.

"You opened the file," the soldier said.

"Exactly," Jayden replied.

"What did you see in it?" Stephen asked.

"There were photos of a person. There were a lot of photos of him. A few photos were of a building named 'The Anti-Plaza FORMULA 1' and there were a few papers. Something about your international villain-y thing-y was written on it. And—"

The soldier interrupted Jayden, "It's the International Supreme Group—"

Jayden shouted, irritated,

"Please soldier-man, you don't have to correct every mistake."

"Sorry, I'll keep that in mind," the soldier said.

"And what happened? What was written on it, did you read it?" Stephen asked.

"Oh, my dear Stephen, by this time you should know that I never read. I think I only read a page or half of that page I think," Jayden explained.

"What was written on it, Jayden? Do you remember at all?" Antonio asked hoping that Jayden would remember something.

"Antonio, I have been stuck with you for 15 years. You know that I can't even remember what I read one week back and you expect me to remember what I read a year ago?" Jayden said.

"No..." Antonio replied, "I expect you to remember for them."

"Alright, fine," Jayden said.

Then Jayden concentrated and tried to remember the details of the file. His brow furrowed and he had a strange expression on his face. He grunted in effort and after five minutes, he relaxed and everyone held their breath in expectation.

And then, those golden words came out of his mouth, "I DON'T REMEMBER ANYTHING."

Frustrated with Jayden, Antonio wanted to hit him now more than ever but he didn't and said, "Let's try one more time."

"No, I think I should head to Satan Lucifer's base. It's probably too late."

By the time Antonio turned around, the archeologist had disappeared.

"Okay, new plan. We need to find the archeologists first," the soldier said.

"Nah! Let them go. What's so important about them?" the soldier said.

"If there is no them, there's no HIDDEN PLACE. Only our leader, the leader of the whole (HOE) HOLDERS OF EARTH, or the archeologists know the exact position of the hidden world. They couldn't have gone far," Stephen said.

"THEY COULDN'T HAVE GONE FAR! What? Are you mad? We've been talking for an hour?"

"As much as I hate eating seals, I hate even more to agree with this guy. But he is right, you have to let it go," Stephen added.

"No, no, no, no. You don't understand. If I don't go with them to Satan Lucifer, he will become suspicious because...because I...I have never done anything that will make him suspicious. This includes killing and thieving from people!"

"WHAT!" Stephen screamed.

"AWESOME!" Jayden said.

Stephen and Antonio looked back at him.

"What? I love action, don't you?" Jayden continued.

Stephen had hardly managed to ignore Jayden, when he said, "Hey! We have to make a plan!"

"Isn't that simple? The soldier will go to Sultan Lucifer or whatever his name is and will think of an excuse that will work for him. In the meanwhile, Stephen will find them and help them. How about that?" Jayden explained.

"I think he is right," Antonio added.

"Alright. I'll head to his base," the soldier said. Suddenly, he heard a huge roar which was getting louder by the minute. When he looked around, he found a polar bear running towards him. He picked up his gun and aimed at it. Jayden immediately shouted, "NO". Both of them stopped at their place. He continued, "Maximus, stop. He is a friend."

"Maximus? Are you serious? You couldn't come up with a better name?" the soldier said.

"No, and he is not an 'it'. 'It' is a he," Jayden explained and the soldier replied "And how do you know that?"

"Because...because he is a male," Jayden replied proudly.

"Of course!" the soldier said slightly peeved.

And when he turned around, Maximus was just an inch away from him. Maximus growled at him and sneezed.

"By the way, we didn't get your name?" Antonio asked.

"Well...for Satan Lucifer I am Zaebos and for the real world I am Adam," He said.

"Well, Adam, so tell us about this plan of yours," Jayden asked.

"Yeah, actually we have it all covered," Adam said.

"No," Stephen said.

"We need you to do something. Which way are you heading?" he asked.

"We are heading south," Antonio replied.

"Good. But you have to head South West. You'll reach a place and between the first two houses, there is telephone booth. Take this coin and put it into the slot. Dial 6006 and as soon as someone picks up, say CODE 100-RED ALARM, repeat it twice," Stephen explained with a serious expression on his face.

"Ok, do you have a compass by any chance?"

"Well, I only have one compass..." Adam said.

"Don't worry. We only need one," Jayden said, walking towards him and snatched the compass out of his hands.

"Let's go, Antonio. We have a lot of work to do."

Both of them hopped onto Maximus's back and disappeared into the dark.

Adam whispered to Stephen, "Where did you find them?"

"Not my choice, Adam," he replied.

Chapter 18

BEN MAKES A DEAL WITH SATAN LUCIFER

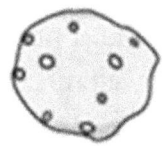

*M*eanwhile, Ben and William were still being held by Satan Lucifer, with no way out.

"Hey, you both!" the guard shouted, "Put on these blindfolds. Sire Satan Lucifer wants to see you."

"So?" William asked.

"So, you have to put on these blindfolds," he replied.

"Why?" William asked.

"So that you are not able to see the way," he replied again.

"See the way? Where are we going?" William asked with wide eyes.

"I have been ordered to take you to Satan Lucifer's court," he replied, peeved.

"Ok," William said.

"Finally—" the guard said, relieved that he wouldn't have to answer any more of William's questions.

"After this final question," William replied.

"WHY...WHY ME?!" he remarked, extremely agonized.

"Because you're the only guard around here," William replied.

"William, shut up and put on your blindfold. Let's go and see what Satan Lucifer wants with us and what he has to say," Ben said.

"We've been walking forever," William whispered, despondently.

"Be patient and keep walking," Ben said, calmly.

It wasn't long till they stopped. Their blindfolds were taken off. The first thing they saw was Satan Lucifer siting right in front of them.

He started speaking immediately, "Well, hello. We meet again. Not by a coincidence this time. You see...I have no interest in killing you. That's why I am offering you a job, here in my palace. You will help me build 'The Thing' I am constructing. After it is finished, I will not only give you freedom, but I will also tell you the way out of this 'Hellhole'. So, do you agree to my terms?" He extended his arm towards Ben to shake his hand as a sign of agreement.

Ben waited for a minute and came closer to him. He whispered in his ears, "I agree to your terms but…I have another favour to ask you…in private, please."

After hearing what Ben had to say, Satan Lucifer snapped his fingers and the four guards left the room?

Satan Lucifer said, "Yes, tell me."

"I only want one thing from you. Can you send a group of soldiers from your triad to find my…to find two children. Their ages are 15 and 17. The older one's height is 5 feet and 9 inches and the younger one is 5 feet and 6 inches. They are both wearing brown jackets. The older one is wearing a green t-shirt and the younger one is wearing a blue t-shirt. If you agree to what I have just said, we'll work for you."

"Well, then. I guess we have a deal," he said.

He shook hands with Ben.

Chapter 19

SARA GETS HELP FROM AIR FORCE

SOS

In Iqualit, Sara was in great panic. She had no news of Ben and her children.

"Oh, God!" She exclaimed. She was extremely frustrated and angry.

She rushed to the Air Force department. She reached there and went to the main control center. She tried to enter but the guard stopped her. He said, "Excuse me, ma'am. You can't be here. You are not allowed here. You have to wait outside."

"NO, I CAN'T," she screamed, tackling him. She ran towards a door on the left. She opened it and saw a man sitting in a chair.

"We have to talk!" she said.

"Wait, ma'am. I am sorry but you are not allowed here," the man said.

"Security!" he shouted, but Sara closed the door and locked it from the inside. He fell on a bench inside the room.

"Look, I don't want to hurt you. I just want talk to you. It's an emergency!" she said, tears streaming down her face. He stood up and let her sit.

He said to her, "Ma'am I am happy to help you, but first I have to settle the people outside right now. Okay?"

She nodded at him. He whispered, "Good."

He opened the door and saw 10 lasers pointed right at him. They were THE RIPD. But in a moment, they recognized that he was not the intruder.

Inside the room, Sara could hear hushed voices from outside. The man told the people that Sara was not a threat. There was nothing to worry about. She just wanted to talk to him.

After some time, he came inside the room and closed the door.

"Have a seat…please," he said, "Now, tell me what happened from the beginning."

Sara sat down and started relating the events of the past few days.

"Five days ago, my children and husband, their step-father, went on a trip to their uncle's house. They left from this heliport. After they took off, I received a call from them. Everyone was very excited. Yesterday, I returned home from the supermarket and tried to call them but they didn't pick up.

I thought they were busy and were probably having fun. But later at night, I tried to call again and they didn't pick up that time either. I tried to call again earlier today, again and again, but they didn't pick up my calls. I even called their uncle. He said that they haven't arrived. I got very worried and I rushed to the flight attendance room. I was told that the helicopter had not returned yet. These are the details of the flight:-

FLIGHT DATE: 18 APRIL
PASSENGERS:
ADULT: BEN LAKE
CHILDREN: ANTONIO SMITH,
                JAYDEN SMITH
RETURN DATE: NOT CONFIRMED

I rushed here immediately because I didn't know where else to go."

"Well, where was the helicopter flying to?" he asked.

"To Annoatok in Greenland," she answered, sniffling.

"Isn't that the city at the very end of Greenland? Well, if we keep going we find ourselves close to the North Pole," he said.

"How many big cities are close to that place?" he asked.

"Around 3-4 cities," she replied.

"But why do you ask?"

"Do you have any photos of them? In your phone or at home?" he asked.

"Yeah, I have their photos," she replied. She opened her purse and after searching through the contents of the bag for some time, she took out her phone and showed him Jayden and Antonio's photos.

"Do you mind?" he asked.

He stood up and went outside the room.

He returned after some time and said, "I have given your phone to the scanning and printing department. They will copy the photos and forward them to the police in the cities closest to Annoatok."

Sara heaved a sigh of relief.

"I am so thankful…" she looked at the badge on his jacket, "Ethan," she said.

She went towards the door. Through the glass pane on the other side, she could see a panel room with a huge antenna on the roof. She turned around.

Ethan asked her, "Any problem ma'am?"

"What's that?" Sara asked, pointing towards the panel.

"Oh that…that's a direction panel room," he said.

"Sorry, I don't understand?" she asked quizzically.

He stood up, came closer to her and started speaking, "Let me explain. For example, if a helicopter or airplane gets lost or loses direction, the panel room knows the exact position of the helicopter or airplane, since the helicopter has a small antenna near the wings. The direction panel room will guide them to the nearest port or safe landing spot."

"Oh!" She exclaimed, "Thanks, Ethan."

As soon as she left Ethan's cabin, she walked a few steps and then she stopped.

"ETHAN!" Sara shouted, opening the door to his cabin.

"I need a favour."

They both headed towards the direction panel room.

"Hey James, get me the information on the last flight of FLIGHT FURY?" Ethan told a person in the panel room.

"It last flew five days ago," James replied.

"Can you track the antenna on it right now,

James? It is urgent," Ethan said.

"Yeah, sure!" he exclaimed.

After some time, James said, "Hey, Ethan. Are you sure the helicopter took off? The antenna is only activated when the helicopter has taken flight. I can't get a location for it or track it. It is possible that the antenna is destroyed or covered with a huge amount of snow."

Hearing this Sara shuddered to think of what might have happened to her family.

"Aren't there any other possibilities?" she asked.

"Well I don't see any other possibilities," James said.

"I…I can't believe that," Sara said with a fake chuckle.

"But wait, if it is covered by snow and if someone manages to brush off the snow, I would be able to get its location," James explained.

"Then, I guess we have to be patient and wait for it," Ethan said looking at James' face.

"I suppose you're right," Sara said.

Chapter 20

THEY FOUND THE FLIGHT FURY

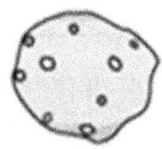

*A*ntonio *and Jayden had set out in search of the telephone booth.*

"Hey, wait," Jayden said. Maximus stopped near a sliding point.

"What!?" Antonio complained.

"Wait! Maximus has to eat. He is a living creature like us," Jayden told him. He opened a bag, took out a fish, and fed it to Maximus.

Antonio felt this was the right time to tell Jayden that he was a foreseer.

"Look Jayden, I want to tell you something. I…I am a foreseer," he said hesitantly.

"Okay…" Jayden spoke slowly.

"No, really. I can prove it to you," Antonio said.

He closed his eyes tightly and forced his mind to see the future.

"Dude, dude. Please tell me, are you trying to prove that you can see the future or are you wasting my time?" Jayden complained.

"Please Jayden trust—" Antonio suddenly stopped speaking. He was having another vision that Jayden was hitting Satan Lucifer with a laser; Stephen, Adam and he were fighting. Maximus was fighting besides them with some other polar bears.

"Jayden, I just had a vision. We were in a crystal cave. You were hitting someone with a locket or something. Adam and Stephen were also there."

"But we have to keep moving, remember what Stephen said."

"Yes, I remember," Jayden said with a sigh.

"Really? Well, can you remind me of the plan?" Antonio asked.

"Yes, of course, why not…sure," Jayden replied, huffing and puffing. He turned his head towards Maximus and whispered to him, "What was the plan?"

Maximus tilted his head in the other direction.

"Yes!" Jayden shouted, "First, we have to head south west…" He put his hand inside his pocket, took out a penny and continued, "Then we will find ourselves near a phone booth. We have to use this penny to make a phone call and say 'CODE 100-RED ALARM'. See, I remember."

Suddenly, Maximus hissed so loudly that the penny fell from Jayden's hand.

"MAXIMUS, YOU SCARED ME!" Jayden shouted but Maximus ignored him.

"YOU DO NOT IGNORE ME!" He furiously yelled again. But Maximus smacked his lips.

"Jayden, Jayden!" Antonio said.

"What is it Antonio? Can't you see I am in the middle of something?" Jayden exclaimed.

"Jayden…the penny, look at the penny," Antonio said.

Both of them stared at the penny as it started sliding away from them.

"NO," Jayden shouted. He jumped to try and stop the penny from slipping away but he wasn't able to save it. The penny kept sliding and sliding and sliding until it hit the ground and suddenly stopped, as if it had hit something metallic.

Jayden dusted his fur coat and went to pick it up. He took it and put it in his pocket but he noticed something else. First, there was a huge amount of snow and the fog was dense. Second, he felt as if there was something behind the fog.

"Jayden, did you get it? Did you save the penny?" Antonio's voice came to Jayden's ears faintly.

"Yes, I have it," shouted Jayden.

"Hey, Antonio. You might want to come down here. I think I found something," Jayden said.

"How should I come down there?" he shouted.

"The same way I did. It is easy. It is painless too," Jayden said.

"Nah I don't think I will! I'll find another way. I can't come down your way," Antonio shouted. Suddenly, Maximus smacked his lips and hugged him from behind. Antonio couldn't handle Maximus' weight. He lost control and fell down from the slide.

Luckily, Maximus had wrapped himself around Antonio, preventing him from getting hurt when he hit the ground.

"Well, at least your landing was soft," Jayden squeaked.

"You think that was soft? I fell 15 feet with Maximus wrapped around me and I could smell nothing but his smell, which is really, really bad," Antonio yelled at him, pacing around in frustration.

"Well, in any case, you landed safely. Besides, look what I found," Jayden said.

"What? A new animal, I suppose?" Antonio complained to him.

"First, that was mean to Maximus. Second, no, it is not an animal. It is something else," Jayden told him and started walking in the other direction.

Meanwhile, Antonio got himself punched in the shoulder by Maximus.

"What!?" Antonio said to Maximus.

"If both of you have had enough fun, maybe we can check what it is there," Jayden said, walking towards the fog.

"Alright, let's go," Antonio said.

"Are you sure you saw something there? We can't see anything here," Antonio said.

"Yes, Antonio, I am sure I saw something," Jayden told him.

Suddenly, Antonio stopped walking.

"What if it is a huge rock?" Antonio said while Jayden was still walking through the fog. By the time he caught up with Jayden, he had disappeared.

"Hey, Jayden! Don't go! Come back here," Antonio shouted.

"Hey, Antonio. Come here," Jayden shouted back.

Without saying anything, Antonio walked towards Jayden. He looked at Jayden and said,

"Jayden I don't think we should get distracted. Let's just do what Stephen told us to do," Antonio said. But Jayden just pointed in the opposite direction.

"Holy Moly…what the…" Antonio whispered. "Is that…is that what I think it is?"

"Yeah, I think it is. It is what we have been looking for since we got here," Jayden said, surprised.

"Yes, it's the helicopter. It's the FLIGHTFURY," Antonio said, walking towards it.

Jayden went to the other side of the helicopter and went inside through the door.

"Antonio, come here. Quickly," Jayden shouted, horrified.

Antonio rushed towards him as fast as could, everything else forgotten. He took a deep breath and said, "What do you think happened, Jayden?"

"Look at this. There is a lot of blood but it is dry, which means it's not fresh. But it also means that either William or Ben was seriously hurt, and by seriously, I mean very, very badly," Jayden said, sitting on his knees.

"How can you tell?" Antonio asked, confused.

"Look, there's blood everywhere. If it had just been a scratch, there would not have been so much blood," Jayden explained.

"But there is another problem," Jayden said.

"And what is that?" Antonio asked.

"Umm…it's my snickers chocolate pack. I can't find it," Jayden said searching the inside of the helicopter frantically.

"Seriously, Jayden we just found out that someone might be badly hurt and you are worried about your snickers chocolate pack?" Antonio complained.

"Never mind…found it," Jayden said, emerging from the helicopter with the packet of snickers in his hand. In the other hand, he was holding a red bag.

"What's in the red bag?" asked Antonio.

"Oh…there are some snacks in it," Jayden said, "And my laptop."

"Your laptop?" Antonio asked, shocked.

"Yeah, it's MY laptop," Jayden replied.

"Jayden are you seriously saying that you have a laptop in your hands right now?" Antonio asked again.

"YES, ANTONIO! The laptop which was invented by Adam Osborne in 1981," Jayden said.

"OPEN IT!" Antonio shouted fiercely.

"Why?" Jayden asked calmly.

"JUST OPEN IT!" Antonio shouted.

"Okay, Okay! Calm down," Jayden said. Jayden put the bag on the ground and took out the laptop. He opened it and said, "Now what?"

"Is anything working? Anything we can use to communicate with mom?" Antonio asked.

"No, it is not possible. There's no network," Jayden explained.

"Oh God! That's bad," Antonio exclaimed. Suddenly, he turned around and said, "Jayden there is one thing…the wire satellite."

"No, Antonio. I may have hacked a lot of things, but I am not going to hack a satellite," Jayden said.

"Jayden, please. What if this is the only chance we have to communicate with mom?" Antonio said.

"We cannot take any more chances or risks," he continued.

"I know, but what is the point if I immediately get arrested when we return home," Jayden said.

"No, you won't get arrested. You're the best hacker I know," Antonio said.

"Because I am the only hacker you know," Jayden replied.

"Yeah, you're probably right," Antonio said, "But that doesn't matter. The important thing is that you're not going to get arrested."

"How do you know?" Jayden asked.

"BECAUSE THEY WOULDN'T EVEN KNOW IT, JAYDEN. PLEASE. THIS MIGHT

BE OUR ONLY CHANCE TO GET BACK HOME," Antonio shouted at the top his voice.

Jayden's eyes were wide open. He stood up, walked the other way, and peeped at Antonio once. He rubbed his face with his palms.

"Okay, I'll do it. But only this once," Jayden said.

Once the windows started, he opened it and there were three apps on the desktop:

1. Aircrack-ng
2. Kali Linux Nethunter.
3. WiFi WPS WPA Satellite HAC

He chose the third one which was called WiFi WPS WPA satellite HAC. He opened it and a web page opened.

"If you don't want to hack a satellite, then why do you have a hacking app for it?" Antonio asked.

"Because I knew if something like this happened, it could be useful and helpful," Jayden replied.

"Yeah, I guess you're right. But how do you even know to hack something?" Antonio asked.

"You remember that I used to go to a robotics club, well actually it wasn't that, it was a hacking session," Jayden replied.

"What! You have been going to hacking sessions for two years?" Antonio cried.

"Yeah! Duh!" Jayden said.

"But you told mom and Ben that you had a robotics class," Antonio said.

"Because they wouldn't have let me go if I had told them it was a hacking class. Do you think they would have let me go?" Jayden replied.

"You are one true evil kid, but also a smart clever kid," Antonio said.

While Jayden did his thingy, Antonio stood up and went inside the helicopter hoping to find something else that might be useful. He looked under the seats but couldn't find anything useful. All he found was junk. He came out from the other end and his eyes fell on a stick. It was the antenna. He picked it up. He suddenly felt as if he was flying in the air but when he turned around, he discovered Maximus holding his t-shirt. Disappointed, he said, "Oh, come on! What did I do now?"

Ignoring him, Maximus hissed and walked towards Jayden. He dropped Antonio like a piece of cake.

"Hey Antonio, you're here already," Jayden said, while munching on his snickers.

"You could have called, you know," Antonio shouted at him furiously.

"Yeah, I know but I didn't. I didn't have to shout because I have my best buddy by my side,"

Jayden said, while hugging Maximus. He kept on munching on his snickers.

"Who's a good boy? Yes you are, yes you are," Jayden said to Maximus.

"Firstly, that is the most disgusting thing I have ever seen. And secondly, any luck with the wire satellite?" Antonio asked. "Yeah, that's why I brought you here. You still have your phone right?" Jayden asked, while munching on his snickers.

"Yeah, I have my phone," Antonio said.

"Great, I need you to open the compass and tell me which way is north," Jayden said while he continued doing something incomprehensible on the laptop and continuously eating his snickers.

"It is that way. Yeah, this way. Face towards your south, that is north," Antonio said.

Jayden said thanks and turned his computer towards the south.

"All right, Whoo! I did it. I hacked it. I hacked the wire satellite," Jayden shouted still having his snickers continuously.

"GOOD, now see if any of the communication apps are working?" Antonio asked.

"Yeah, sure," Jayden said.

"OH NO, NO, NO, NO, NO, this can't be happening right now!" Jayden cried in extreme agony.

"What happened?" Antonio asked, shocked, even though he didn't know what had happened,

"I am all out of snickers," Jayden shouted, trying to look for any snickers that he might have missed.

But he didn't find anything. At least, that's what Antonio thought.

"Ha! Got you, I am just messing with you," Jayden said, chuckling.

"Jayden, c'mon! Are you seriously kidding me?!" Antonio yelled at him.

Jayden turned back to his laptop. That's when he got the really bad news.

"Uh...Antonio we...we have a problem," Jayden said.

"Jayden, stop being annoying. You've already played a trick on me once. I am not going to fall for your silly jokes...." Antonio replied.

"But the laptop..." Jayden had almost finished his sentence when Antonio interrupted him and started walking the opposite way.

"What, Jayden? You're gonna say that the laptop is fused, or it's destroyed or something like that, right?"

"It's neither of those things. It is dead," Jayden said.

"Say, what!" Antonio said. He turned around and checked the laptop.

"OH, NO, NO, NO!!!" Antonio cried in extreme agony.

"Why do these things keep happening to us?"

"Because we're trapped here, in the North Pole, I guess," Jayden squeaked so slowly that Antonio could hardly hear him.

"I did not ask for your opinion," Antonio said abruptly.

"Okay, I am out," Jayden said putting his hands up in the air.

Suddenly they felt a quake.

"Hey, Antonio! Did you feel that as well?" Jayden asked.

"Yeah, I felt it. Is it an earthquake?"

"NO, it is not a natural earthquake," Antonio replied.

Although the earth below them stopped shaking, a huge chunk of ice from the glacier overhead fell close to them.

"How can you say that?" Jayden asked quizzically.

"Well, actually, a real earthquake would cause more damage than this one," Antonio explained.

"Maybe this was a small one," Jayden said.

"No, if it had been a small earthquake, it wouldn't have caused this much damage. Well, if we look at it objectively, it is too much damage for a small earthquake but not enough damage for a large earthquake," Antonio said.

Suddenly, they felt another quake rumble through the earth. But this wasn't a quake. It was as if something very, very heavy had fallen on the surface.

"It was so…different this time. It is not a fake quake this time for sure," Jayden exclaimed.

"No, it's a…ROCK!!!" Antonio yelled.

Their eyes fell on a gigantic rock that was rolling towards them at full speed. That's when Maximus came to the rescue. He ran up the slope as fast as he could to try and stop the rock.

Antonio ran towards Jayden who was running in the opposite direction. But it was too late. The rock hit the helicopter fuel tank, which started leaking and suddenly they heard a loud noise. BOOM!

The explosion made Antonio and Jayden fly across to the other side. They fainted as they hit the ground. Maximus too was stuck in a large snowball as he slid down the slope. He tried to stop the descent but he couldn't control his speed.

The loud sound attracted a group of Satan Lucifer's soldiers who had been nearby. They quickly rushed to find the source of the sound. They found Antonio, Jayden and Maximus there.

They captured them.

"Uh…what happened?" Jayden said weakly.

He realized that he was in a cage. He saw Antonio lying beside him. Maximus was trapped in a steel cage as well.

"Maximus!" He shouted.

"Rest. You are in no condition to speak," a black man said.

After a little while, Jayden's eyes closed. He had fainted again.

Chapter 21

BEN'S GOTTA LIVE
UP TO HIS DEAL

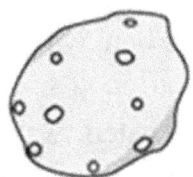

At the Vampire headquarters, Antonio and Jayden found themselves trapped in a cage.

"UH…my head is whirling," Antonio said, shaking his head.

"Oh, you're up," the guard said.

Antonio realized that he was locked in a cage. He started to panic and asked the guard, "Where am I? Where is my brother? Where is my brother's pet? Where's my brother's body? Where is my brother? Tell me! Where is my brother? I need to see him," Antonio shouted

"General, where is the report from the practice test yesterday?" Satan Lucifer asked the General.

"Positive, sire. The practice test yesterday was a total success," the general replied.

"What if...General," Satan Lucifer said getting up from his throne

✡ ✡ ✡

"Relax. Look behind you. You have been unconscious for so long, yet you have so much energy left in you," the guard said.

Antonio saw Jayden lying unconscious and rushed towards him.

"Hey, Jayden...Jayden, wake up... come on, open your eyes," Antonio said, holding him in his arms.

He looked here and there for any supplies. He was content simply to discover a mug of water on the side. He took it and splashed some water on Jayden's face.

"HUH! What happened, Antonio?" Jayden asked, shaking his head.

"I don't remember clearly," Antonio replied.

Suddenly, they heard a loud drumming. The sound was getting louder and louder by the minute.

"HIRE SIRE!" cried every guard, including the guard who was standing outside Antonio and Jayden's cage.

Satan Lucifer stopped right in front of Antonio and Jayden's cage.

As soon as Jayden saw Satan Lucifer, he had a strange feeling about him. It felt like he had seen him somewhere but he wasn't sure because everything seemed to be a blur. He didn't say anything.

Satan Lucifer stepped ahead and said, "Well, if it isn't the newest member of the crew."

"What do you mean? Where are we?" Antonio asked him, standing up.

"Ah so many questions…" he said.

"He only asked two questions… duh!" Jayden said.

Satan Lucifer did not pay any attention to him.

"You were brought here for a purpose," Satan Lucifer said.

"Oh, yeah? And what purpose is that?" Antonio asked

"I…perhaps…well, it's because of someone who claims to be your father or your step-dad, to be more specific," Satan Lucifer said.

"Ben!" Antonio whispered.

Jayden stood up using all his might, and walked towards the cage's railing.

Satan Lucifer told a guard to bring Ben and William. Ben shook off the guard and ran towards them.

"Antonio! Jayden! Are you both alright?" Ben asked with a happy expression on his face.

"We are both fine. What are you doing here?" Jayden asked, worryingly.

"Ah…it's a very long story," William said.

That's when a guard came running. He was heaving and could barely speak.

"Sire…sire, I come with great news and grave news…our minister, Zaebos, has discovered the location of the hidden world with the help of the archeologist. The grave news is that our minister is hurt and all the other soldiers are missing. He is saying that someone attacked them," the guard said.

Hearing this, Satan Lucifer ordered all the guards to gather in the court where Adam (Zaebos) was.

Antonio and Jayden looked at each other's faces. Both of them wore worried expressions. Since they had all been ordered to gather in the court, a guard shut Ben and William in Antonio and Jayden's cage.

"What happened out there, dear Zaebos?" Satan Lucifer asked.

"I don't remember exactly, but we were not far from here, about five miles or so. We were attacked by a pack of animals. Our soldiers died but I survived," Adam told Satan Lucifer.

"General, is it ready?" Satan Lucifer asked, looking at the General.

"Sire, I'm afraid it might take..." the General started speaking, but Satan Lucifer interrupted him and shouted fiercely, "IS IT READY OR NOT, ANSWER ME WITH A YES OR NO!"

"Yes, yes, certainly, my lord," the General said, terrified.

"Good. We head to the hidden world tonight," Satan Lucifer said, walking towards his throne.

"Bring out the prisoners," Satan Lucifer told a guard.

The guard came with all four of them--William, Ben, Antonio and Jayden.

"What are you going to do to us?" Ben asked.

"I want you all to work for me. I don't know who you are, or where you are from, but what I do know is if you continue to work for me, I will set you free," Satan Lucifer said.

"And why would we want to work for you?" William asked.

"Ooh, ooh I know what will happen now, this man sitting here will say..." Jayden said, walking in front of William and pointing towards Satan Lucifer. He had barely begun his sentence, when he suddenly stopped. As soon as he saw the shining emerald stone in Satan Lucifer's armor, Jayden had a sudden realization.

"Well if you have finished speaking, you will be told about your work tomorrow. You will start tomorrow," Satan Lucifer said.

Chapter 22

RESCUE MISSION TEAM

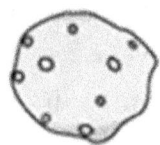

In Iqualit, Ethan and Sara were sitting in the navigation room.

"ETHAN!!! I think there is a signal here. Ethan, come here," James shouted.

Sara and Ethan rushed to James.

"What happened? Can you receive the signal?" Ethan asked.

"Yes. The helicopter's location was displayed on the screen a few minutes ago," James said.

"So? Where are they? Where are my kids and husband?" Sara asked.

"They…" James said and peeped into the screen. He turned around with a horror struck expression and said, "They…they are at the North Pole!"

"C'mon! This is serious! I know you like to play pranks, but we're talking about the life of two kids here," Ethan said.

"Oh yeah? Come here and see for yourself. Look at the location," James said, pushing his chair away from his computer.

"Psst...fine...I'll check for myself," Ethan said confidently, stepping ahead, only to find himself staring into James' eyes.

"Uh...the computer is there," James said awkwardly.

"Oh...right!" Ethan said.

Sara was slowly becoming impatient, and she shouted at them, "Just get it over with, you two."

Ethan looked at the computer and realized that James was right.

"Uh...see? I was right. It is just 300 km away from Annoatok."

"And where does it end..." murmured James to himself, "It ends...ooh you are right. Sara I think that James is right. Your family is at the North Pole," Ethan said

"THEN GET THEM OUT OF THERE!" shouted Sara, holding Ethan's arms and shaking him.

"Well Sara...I will need some time to get together a team for this rescue mission," Ethan said.

"Fine. Take as much as time as you need but get them out of there," Sara replied

It took Ethan about half an hour to gather a team for the rescue mission.

"Hello, Sara. Meet our cold region air force commander. He will lead the rescue mission," Ethan said. He introduced Sara to a tall, handsome man who was wearing a white leather armor over a blue uniform.

He stepped forward and said, "Hello, ma'am. I am Captain Rogers. I am the leader of the rescue mission. This is my squad." Sara saw five officers, wearing blue uniforms, standing behind him. They were holding their helmets on the side and were attempting to make a rather dramatic entrance.

"Tell them to stop making their dramatic entrance. It's killing me," Sara whispered softly.

"Hey, guys..." Captain Rogers shouted, "She isn't buying it. Come here, quickly."

"Aww man! She's the first person who's not buying it," one of the crew members said.

"Yeah, neither did the previous 28 people," said one of the female crew members.

"Ssh, you guys!" another crew member said.

"Let me introduce them:

Bruno, Katie, Alex and, Alexandra," Captain Roger said while pointing to each of the crew members.

"Glad to meet you," Sara said, "But Ethan, how will you find them?" Sara asked.

"Leave that to us. If the pilot is alive, the chances of finding them are higher," Ethan explained.

"Sir, the helicopter is ready," a pilot shouted from behind.

"Captain Rogers, please bring them back safely," Sara said.

"This is what we're trained to do, ma'am," Captain Rogers said.

Chapter 23

THE PLATINUM LOCKET

*A*t Satan Lucifer's headquarters, plans were underway to locate and enter the hidden city.

Adam was walking past the dungeon where Antonio and Jayden had been locked up. He was stunned. He ran up to them and said, "Hey... psst...hey."

Antonio saw him and said, "Adam, you're here!"

"Yeah, but you're not supposed to be here. You were supposed to make the emergency phone call," Adam said.

"How are we supposed to do that when we are stuck here?" Jayden spoke from behind.

"Hey, get away from my children!" Ben shouted furiously.

"Ben, calm down. He's a good guy. He's with us," Antonio said.

"It's a long story," Jayden said.

"You can tell us now. It's not like we are going anywhere," William said.

"Yes, you are," Adam said, taking out a set of keys from his pocket.

He opened the locker and said, "Come on, go. You gotta go. Get the code to them."

Although, they got out of the dungeon, they lost the way. Suddenly, Jayden saw a silver container and started walking towards it. He saw a railing and tried to look inside it. He whispered, "Hello, anybody in there."

"I see worth in you. You are the one who will be able to kill him. Take this platinum locket and finish him. But you must remember that this should not fall in the wrong hands. And remember, only you can unlock the locket's power. When all hope is lost, take this locket and point it towards Satan Lucifer and press it. But you must understand that you are holding the power to save everyone. In the darkest time, it burns the brightest. You have to stay back, no matter what. Don't leave this place. One more thing, your father was investigating this organization. Maybe your father's death wasn't a coincidence," a man's voice came out of the steel box. A hand appeared, reaching through the railing and pressed the locket into his hands.

"How do you know my father? I have seen this locket in a photo but I don't quite remember it," Jayden said.

"Let's just say…I have sources."

Jayden was hesitant to take the locket, but finally, he took it and ran back to the others. He wore it around his neck and tucked it under his shirt so no one would be able to see it. Although, he still wasn't sure about the locket, he decided to keep it.

"Let's go, Jayden. We have to get them the code," Antonio said.

"Maybe, we should stay here to make sure that Satan Lucifer is not able to accomplish his plans," Jayden said.

"Well that won't be necessary. Once you get this code to HOE, they will take care of everything," Adam said.

"Yeah, what happened? Why are we turning back now?" Antonio said.

"No, we have to stay back for some reason," Jayden said.

"What's gotten into you, Jayden? We are so close now. We can't turn back now," Antonio insisted.

"I remember, Antonio. Now I remember it all. Somehow, I think dad's death was not accidental. I have to find out what happened." Jayden said, "And I might even know how to defeat Satan Lucifer."

They were interrupted by the sound of loud drums, "Oh no, they're going to the location. Quick, into the bushes," Adam said.

"Okay, new plan. Antonio, Jayden and I will stay back while both of you will go and find a phone booth and dial 6006 CODE 100-RED ALARM," he told Ben and William.

"Here, take this penny. You'll need it," Antonio said.

"Wait! I am not going without you. I will stay with you," Ben said.

"Ben, please. I have already lost one father. I can't bear to lose another," Jayden said.

Ben and William nodded.

"You'll have to head South West," Adam said, checking his compass.

"Adam, where's Maximus?" Jayden cried.

"They must have locked him in the dungeon for animals," Adam exclaimed.

"What you're waiting for? They have already started moving. We must free him," Antonio said.

As Satan Lucifer had taken all of his guards and soldiers with him, they had an advantage.

When they entered the animal dungeon, they saw many animals of every kind.

"It will take up so much time to find him in here," Jayden complained.

"No, it won't. Your polar bear was the last animal who was imprisoned here. He's probably at the very end," Adam said.

They found Maximus's cage but they also found padlock on it.

"Oh, c'mon! When did villains start using complex technologies," Antonio said, irritated.

"Quick. Find something we can use to break this lock," Adam said.

Jayden remembered the locket he had. He took it out, pointed it towards the locker, and pressed a button. A laser came out from the locket, and it completely destroyed the lock.

"Hey guys, come here, I broke it," he shouted.

By the time Adam and Antonio came over, the lock was burned.

Adam found it suspicious, but he didn't say anything.

"Come on, hop on," Jayden said.

"I've never ridden a polar bear," Adam said.

"And now you will," Jayden said.

"Maybe it will be fun," Adam said.

"AAAHHHH!!!! STOP THIS FEROCIOUS BEAST," Adam shouted but his voice was lost in the wind.

"Maximus, slow down, we can see them," Antonio said lightly.

Maximus slowed down. Adam got off him and ran behind a tree. "Hey, bud what are you doing?" Antonio asked Adam.

"I just threw up. I was feeling very nauseous," Adam said.

Jayden screwed up his face as if he was going to throw up as well.

"Adam, why are they here at the sea point?" Jayden asked.

"Do you remember what Stephen said? He mentioned that the hidden place is underwater and comes out once every ten years," Adam explained.

"General, bring out the divers," Satan Lucifer told the general.

Six divers walked to the edge of the sea. Ten people emerged from the back of a truck and took out the dynamite.

The general said, "Sire, this Dynamite can only be lifted by ten people but there are only six divers. Will they be able to manage?"

"Yes, general. The dynamite's cover is made up of chemicals. It will be much lighter in the water," Satan Lucifer explained.

***

"What should we do now?" asked Jayden.

"It has only been three minutes, man! You are so impatient," Adam said.

"Yeah, I know. I have been told that many times," Antonio said.

"We need to wait now," Adam said.

Chapter 24

CODE RECEIVED

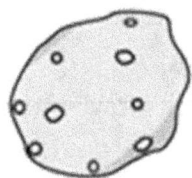

Meanwhile, Ben and William had managed to locate a phone booth.

"Ben...Ben, can you see the phone booth? I can see the phone booth," William said.

"Yes, I see it William," Ben replied.

They both ran towards it. As soon as they went closer, they were able to see a house close to the phone booth. By the time they reached the phone booth, they realized they had stumbled into a village.

"WHOA!" William exclaimed.

"Yeah, WHOA!" Ben added.

They headed towards the booth.

"Here, hand me the penny," Ben said. William took out the penny from his coat and handed it over to him.

Ben dialed 6006. A man picked up and said, "Welcome to the council of municipality. How can I help you?"

"CODE 100-RED ALARM, CODE 100-RED ALARM," Ben said.

Ben waited for a while but he couldn't hear anyone on the other end, so he hung up.

"Now what?" William asked.

"Now we go to the kids," Ben said decisively.

"Yes, let's go," William replied.

Chapter 25

THEY DEFEAT SATAN LUCIFER

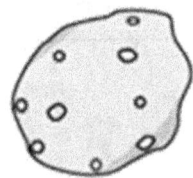

Jayden couldn't take his eyes off the locket. He was amazed by its powers. Maximus was sitting beside him and eating a fish.

He suddenly felt the earth shake.

"Was that an earthquake?" Antonio asked.

"No," Adam replied, "It's the hidden world rising to the surface."

Satan Lucifer put his hand in the air and closed it. The door of an armed car opened and a guy in handcuffs stepped out. Satan Lucifer ordered the divers to go into the sea with the dynamite.

"When do we attack?" Jayden asked.

"Now is not the right time. We have to let them go inside. Once they are inside, they won't be able to get out," Adam explained.

"Adam is right. We should wait," Stephen said from behind.

"Stephen, you scared us half to death," Antonio yelled at him.

"What are you doing here?" Adam asked.

"The whole North Pole felt that quake. I did too and saw both of you, but where's Jayden?" Stephen asked.

"I am right here," Jayden said.

"Where have you been?" Antonio asked.

"I was keeping an eye on them, waiting for our cue," Jayden said, "I hope you brought your guns. We will probably need them now."

"Adam, look. The hidden place has risen from the ocean," Stephen said, shocked.

The hidden place was as huge as a palace. They had to walk two kilometers to get to where the guardians stood.

Satan Lucifer and his army led the handcuffed man towards the entrance.

"Stephen, Adam, Antonio, they have started. We should start moving too," Jayden said.

"I agree," Stephen said, "Let's move."

"Let's go already," Antonio said and climbed on Maximus' back. Jayden chuckled and sat on Maximus' back as well.

"Anyone else wants a ride too?" Jayden asked.

"Nah, I am good," Adam said.

"I prefer to walk as well," Stephen said.

"Come on, stand on the line," Satan Lucifer said, pushing the handcuffed man towards the line. A soldier held him still on the line. As soon as he stood on the line, the guardians stood up. They were 18 feet tall. They lifted their spears up and slammed them into the ground which made it difficult for the divers to attach the dynamite below the hidden world.

"Great, we took the long way to get to here, and now, we have to walk two miles to get there," Jayden said, irritated.

They had almost reached Satan Lucifer and his army, when suddenly, everybody started disappeared.

"Where are they disappearing?" Antonio asked.

"They are not going anywhere. We just can't see them, neither can they see us," Stephen explained.

They emerged out of a bush. One by one, all the soldiers went inside through the hidden entrance. The guard who was holding the handcuffed prisoner went inside with him.

"Should we go inside now?" Antonio asked.

Adam nodded in agreement.

Stephen put his leg inside. A force field appeared and hit him so hard that he flew ten meters away.

"How could I forget that, jeez?" Adam said, very angry with himself.

"What should we do now?" Antonio asked confusedly.

"We have to wait for them. There is nothing we can do about this," Stephen said, limping all the way to them.

The three of them started walking back but Jayden stayed.

"Guardians, Sir, I don't know anything about you or what this is all about but one of the men who has just gone inside killed my father. I have to get justice. He took the life of the person I loved the most in this world, please," he said, kneeling in front of the Guardians.

"Come on, Jayden. It's not going to work," Antonio said and continued walking.

As soon as Jayden stood up, the locket slipped out of his shirt, and the guardians recognized it immediately. They stood up and hit their spears on the ground and kneeled before him. The other three turned around and saw that the force field was no more. Jayden stood in the line while

Antonio, Stephen and Adam went through the entrance.

"Hey, 'S'. What's up? Ready to face jail?" Antonio said, making a dramatic entrance.

"Don't call me that. How did you manage to enter?" Satan Lucifer shouted.

"Guess they don't only allow the chosen person to enter," Jayden said with open arms and the Guardians behind him.

They saw that the hidden world was made up of crystals. There were three stones in the center that were glowing as bright as the sun.

The soldiers started firing their guns, but the guardians covered them.

"FIRE!" Jayden shouted.

Fire ensued from the hands of the Guardians.

"WATER!" Jayden shouted again.

The other guardian spurted a huge amount of water from his mouth. But nothing affected Satan Lucifer. Adam was firing with his gun. Stephen was shooting with his gun as well. But the bullets just passed through him. Maximus was punching everyone. He roared furiously and after a minute a whole sleuth came roaring into the cave. The polar bear in the middle was huge.

Jayden saw that Satan Lucifer was fighting.

He took the locket and at the right moment, he aimed the locket at Satan Lucifer. Satan Lucifer stumbled.

"That weapon," Satan Lucifer said, "Give it to me."

Jayden pressed the locket again, preventing Satan Lucifer from running away. He didn't take his finger off the locket.

"Did you kill Anthony Thomas?" Jayden shouted angrily.

"Yeah, that man almost discovered our secret plan. I gave him a horrible death," Satan Lucifer said.

Jayden pressed the locket with all his strength and a huge laser beam hit Satan Lucifer.

Suddenly, Antonio joined him and added his strength to Jayden's. Both of them pressed the locket with all their might, and finally it stopped Satan Lucifer's army. All his soldiers were either dead or had fainted. The laser stopped everyone.

Jayden fell to his knees and saw that the armor had been completely destroyed. The stone flew through the air and became embedded in the walls with the other sacred stones.

But they had forgotten about something— the Dynamite. There was a huge explosion. The explosion was so huge that it generated a large tsunami.

They ran back as the hidden place started to sink back into the ground. Everyone hopped onto Maximus' back and on the other polar bear's back. He ran as fast as he could. They got out just in time. The long path that led to the hidden place sank with it.

They all got off Maximus and looked back. There was no sign of the hidden city. Suddenly, Satan Lucifer came out of the water and attacked them but Maximus punched him and roared at him.

"At last, this ferocious beast was useful."

They all felt the earth tremble.

"What was that?" Antonio asked.

They all turned around to find themselves in a whirlpool of dust.

Just then, they saw five helicopters heading their way. Another helicopter was coming from the opposite direction.

The helicopters hovered above them and a rope ladder was thrown down so that they climb up it.

"That helicopter belongs to the HOE, but I don't know which organization that helicopter belongs to," said Stephen.

"WHO ARE YOU?" shouted Antonio.

"We are from the Air Force. We have been ordered to rescue you by your mother Sara," shouted Captain Rogers on the speaker.

Antonio quickly climbed up the ladder into the air force helicopter. Just as Jayden was about to step on the ladder, Maximus held him back.

"No, bud. You can't come with me, you belong here," Jayden explained with tears in his eyes. Maximus had helped him so much on this adventure. He would miss Maximus so much. Maximus put his huge paws around Jayden and hugged him. Then, he slowly made his way back into the forest.

Adam took Satan Lucifer and climbed into the HOE helicopter.

"Where is your father?" asked captain Rogers.

"Hey, here. Look down here," Ben shouted.

Antonio and Jayden threw down a ladder. William and Ben climbed the ladder and came up.

Ben saw a hand reaching out towards him. He looked up and saw Antonio.

"Come on, man. Don't make it weird," he said.

They all had a good chuckle.

"Hey! Are you alright, Mr. William," asked the pilot.

"Yeah, I am fine," William said.

"I could use a pair of extra hands, you know," the pilot said. Without saying anything, William went and sat down beside the other pilot.

"Well I guess you are a foreseer after all," Jayden said.

Antonio chuckled and replied, "Yeah…"

Chapter 26

HOME SWEET HOME

They finally reached Iqualit, after collecting their awards for bravery in Annoatok.

They headed towards their house slowly. They were tired and exhausted from their adventure. They saw their home coming closer and closer until they finally realized they were standing right in front of their house. They stood in front of the door, hesitant to ring the bell. However, before they could ring the doorbell, the door opened and they saw Sara standing right in front of them. They were all standing outside until Jayden said, "Want a hug?"

Without wasting a moment, Sara hugged both of them.

"Let's go inside," she said.

***

At night, during dinner Sara asked them about their adventure.

"So, did you enjoy your time together?" Sara asked.

"Well, it was hard in the beginning, but it ended well," Antonio said, looking towards Ben.

"Yeah, we really enjoyed it," Jayden added.

Suddenly, they heard the doorbell ring. Jayden got up and opened the door. He shouted excitedly, "Mom, its aunt Olivia and uncle John."

Everyone got up from their seats and ran towards the door.

They greeted Olivia and John, and led them to the living room.

All of them sat down on the sofa near the fireplace and Antonio asked, "Aunt Olivia, what did you bring for us?"

"What? A good and exciting adventure with a happy ending isn't enough for you?" she asked.

Everyone started laughing. They hadn't had a good laugh in a really long time.

THE END

Questions From The Story

Let's see how carefully you have read this book

Q1: What was ben's occupation?
- (A) successful businessman
- (B) successful husband
- (C) successful ice hockey player
- (D) successful stepdad

Q2: Which helicpoter were they going to ride?
- (A) flight fury
- (B) sonic machine
- (C) thunder ranger
- (D) burning sun

Q3: What did Mr. William want to become?
- (A) teacher
- (B) pilot
- (C) ice hockey player
- (D) doctor

Q4: What was jayden's secret?
- (A) he liked ben
- (B) he didn't like sherlock holmes
- (C) he was a hacker
- (D) he had a locket that could destroy satan lucifer.

Q5: Who were the five main characters in this story?

(A) antonio, jayden, ben, stephen, adam

(B) antonio, jayden, ben, william, stephen

(C) antonio, jayden, ben, sara, william

(D) antonio, jayden, ben,satan lucifer, william

www.ingramcontent.com/pod-product-compliance
Lightning Source LLC
Chambersburg PA
CBHW052000220626
47052CB00004B/1021

* 9 7 8 9 3 8 8 4 9 7 8 6 2 *